I0519704

Also by James Castagno

Octavia and the Greek Key

The Lady of the Lantern

Dance of the Red Panel

Witness to Terror

Fugitive Series Book One

Out of Tunis

Fugitive Series Book Two

Out of Naples

Fugitive Series Book Three

COME NEMESIS

James Castagno

A Novella

Come Nemesis is a work of fiction. All characters, businesses, places, events or incidents either are the products of the author's imagination or are used fictitiously. Any resemblance to actual persons, living or dead, or actual events and locales is purely coincidental.

Behold on wrong swift vengeance waits and art subdues the strong.

The Odyssey of Homer

– Alexander Pope

CHAPTER I

PAIN AND PLEASURE

Thirty-five-year-old Mike Anello leapt out of bed. With a distinct limp, he ran from his dark room. "Quick. Get out!" he screamed.

Wide eyes scanned the entire living room on his way to the front door. He yanked it open and stepped onto the front porch of his modern log home.

Mike stood in his underwear, surveyed the yard, and looked for approaching danger among the moonlit trees and winding driveway. His heart pounded. He took a deep breath and shivered when he felt the cool air contact his sweat covered body. To his right he focused on the floodlight beside his neighbor's garage door, fifty yards from his house. He ducked behind the railing and watched a man in a full length, long-sleeved thawb, and a black and white headscarf, bury something beside his neighbor's wall. *An improvised explosive.* His right hand groped for his rifle, but made contact with nothing.

Adrenalin pumped through his body. A pain shot through his scarred left leg and he glanced back toward the neighbor's garage. The man was no longer there. Mike shook his head, looked at his underwear and bare legs, as he rubbed the side of his thigh and calf. *Remember what they told you. This is Colorado not Afghanistan... it's not real.*

Mike raised both arms above his head, took a deep breath, and gazed at the stars. The silence of the night brought him back to reality. *When is this going to stop?* He headed back into the house.

In the living room, he turned on a table lamp and pulled a pair of sweatpants from the back of the couch. As he sat, his fingers ran along the wide scars covering his left leg. *Looks like hell... at least they saved it.* He slipped into the pants and walked into the kitchen.

At the sink he wet a dish towel and wiped the perspiration from his hands, chest and face. A short toss sent the cloth into the sink. He turned down a hallway, opened a steel door, and entered a bedroom devoid of any semblance of comfort. Under the opened curtains, thick metal bars covered the two windows.

A double barrel shotgun, a vintage AR-15 rifle, and a HK 416 assault rifle stood inside a tall, glass-fronted, oak gun cabinet. Mike stepped in front of an eight-foot long table in the center of the room. He looked at a dissembled rifle, Leupold Mark 8 scope, and a ten inch Titan suppressor. A cleaning rod, oil and stained cloths lay to the side. Against a wall across the room, a reloading press stood on a counter above three cabinets.

It took him less than five minutes to assemble the weapon and attach the scope. He picked up the forty-nine inch long Barrett .338 Lapua Magnum and examined the sniper rifle. He placed the rifle and suppressor in a long black gun case on the floor, cringed and pressed his hand against his thigh. *Damn it hurts. Shouldn't have jumped out of bed so fast.*

Eight large framed photos, and a larger framed white parchment hanging on the wall caught his eye. He walked to them and looked at the pictures of him and his spotter, Dave, in Afghanistan. He shook his head. The parchment next to them was a quote by Alexander Pope that had been penned in bold calligraphy. Next to it hung a plaque from the Special Operations Warrior Foundation.

He seldom looked at the wall. The images took him back to the day Dave was shot in the head and his brains splattered across Mike's cheek. He turned to focus on Pope's quote and read it aloud. "Behold on wrong swift vengeance waits; and art subdues the strong."

Thirty minutes later he had showered, dressed and set the breakfast dishes and a coffee cup in the sink. In the living room he picked up a backpack and the black rifle case on his way to the door. He turned on the alarm system and headed to his Jeep Wrangler.

It took an hour for him to leave civilization behind. He turned onto a dirt road and started up a dry treeless hill.

After fifteen minutes bouncing in the driver's seat, he stopped the Jeep, got out, and placed five plastic jugs of water, a yard apart, at the side of the road. A three-inch red circle had been painted on each container. He returned to the Jeep, shifted into four wheel drive, and continued uphill. When he reached a half mile from the jugs, he pulled to the side and stopped.

Long distance shooting... love it. Cleaning is a pain in the ass. He set his rifle on a beach towel, brushed dirt from a corner of the towel and attached the suppressor to the barrel. From his backpack he removed a twelve-inch tripod and screwed a Bushnell range finder onto it.

Mike's first shot hit a yard to the side and a foot in front of the left jug. He made two minor adjustments on the scope and aimed at the same red circle. *Relax, take your time and control your breathing.* He squeezed the trigger. The jug exploded. In the next forty-five seconds he fired four times without missing a container.

He smiled, leaned to his range finder and focused on the damp ground where the containers had once stood.

Damn, a smidgen over a half mile. Still got it. "I'll add a quarter mile tomorrow."

With a satisfying grin, he placed his rifle in the case, dug his keys out of his pocket and drove home.

CHAPTER II

THE NEWS

Mike turned into his driveway, removed his mail from the box, and then continued to the house.

After he unpacked his gun case and backpack in the secure room, he sat on the couch and opened an envelope from Charles Schwab. *Nine hundred grand... thirty four thousand in checking. Thank God for the olive oil business.* When he dropped the pages on the coffee table, his cell phone rang. He pulled it from his pocket and looked at name on the screen.

"Hi Gina. How's my favorite cousin in Italy?"

"Not well." Her voice cracked. "And Mike, I'm your only cousin."

He sat up straight. "What's wrong? Are you crying?"

"Yes." She sobbed. "My father is dead!"

Mike's eyes widened, and he leapt off the couch. "Jesus! What the hell happened?"

Gina's sobbing and crying kept her from continuing. Mike recognized the voice of his uncle's business manager.

"Mike, its Pio Baldi."

"Damn, Pio. What happened to my uncle? How did he die?"

"He didn't just die, Mike."

Mike furrowed his brow. "Gina said he did! What's going on over there?"

"Your uncle was murdered."

Mike froze, stared at the floor and rubbed his forehead. "Murdered?" He yelled. "How the hell... how and who killed him?"

"We're not sure who did it, but we know why. Your cousin needs help. Can you come here?"

"I decided to do that when you told me how he died. I'll be there as soon as possible. Why was he murdered?" He waited for a response. "Pio?"

"Yes, Mike. It's a long story that your uncle didn't want to tell you. He thought he could fix the problem, but now we may lose the business."

Mike shook his head and lowered his voice. "Why was he killed, Pio?"

"For the past two years a crime family demanded monthly payments. They said it's a business protection fee. Every six months the amount increased until finally Romeo couldn't afford to pay them."

Mike tightened his jaw. "Who are these people?"

Pio lowered his voice to a whisper. "You need to talk to Gina. Tell her you are coming and I'll explain everything when you get here. I paid the men yesterday. They won't bother us for a month."

"Okay, I'll call you later. Like I said, I'll get there as soon as I can, but it might take a few days to settle everything here. Make sure Gina is safe. Let me speak to her."

While he waited for his cousin, Mike thought about the terrible news and mumbled. "If there's a problem, why have my quarterly checks been the same?" It broke his train of thought when he heard Gina's voice.

"What did you say, Mike?"

"Nothing. I'll leave here as soon as I can and fly into Reggio Calabria. Don't worry about meeting me at the airport or train station. I'll get to the house."

"Thank you," Gina said. "I'm sorry I called with bad news."

"If you didn't call, I would be angry. Will you be okay until I get there?

"Yes. You'll miss my father's funeral."

Mike took a deep breath. "I know, but I'm alone and need to make plans so I can stay for a while. Tell Pio I don't want either of you to say anything to the police about the payments. We'll figure out what to do when I get there."

"Okay. Come as fast as you can."

"I will. I love you." He ended the call, clamped his teeth together, and shook his head.

CHAPTER III

PREPARATION

For the next three days Mike stayed in contact with his cousin by email and text messages while making arrangements for what he knew would be an extended trip to Italy.

He removed three rifles and six pistols from his gun cabinet and set them on the cleaning table. Each weapon was then placed into a separate Pelican gun case.

Mike carried the gun cases to his Jeep, set them in the back beside a gray twelve-inch-long plastic container, and returned to the house. In the living room he slung an army rucksack over his shoulder, extended the handle of a rigid carry-on suitcase and picked up the sniper rifle case. He pressed his lips together and looked around the room, not sure when he'd return. The quiet five acres of land in the hills outside Colorado Springs was a place he had come to heal and reflect on his time in the army. He shook his head, turned on the house alarm, and locked the door.

The drive to his friend's house in Colorado Springs took an hour. Mike pulled into the driveway of the two-story brick house, walked to the front door and rang the bell.

Bob Keal opened the door. "Come in, Mike. Sorry to hear the bad news."

On their way to the living room, Bob called his wife. "Julie! Mike is here."

Mike met Bob six years earlier while both were stationed with the 1st Battalion, 503rd Parachute Infantry Regiment in Vicenza, Italy. Bob had been the unit's armorer, and a former sniper.

They stepped into the living room and sat.

"How did your uncle die?" Bob asked.

"Heart attack. We didn't expect it. He worked like a dog and seemed to be in great shape."

When Julie entered the room, Mike stood and hugged her.

"Sorry about your uncle," she said.

"Thank you. I'm going there for a few months to see if I can help out."

She nodded. "I'll put lunch together while you and Bob talk."

After Julie left the room, Mike took a deep breath, and looked at Bob. "I want to thank you for taking care of my guns while I'm gone."

"You'd do the same for me."

Mike smiled. "You know I would. I spoke with Frank Weatherbee in Vicenza. He said you guys stay in close contact."

"Yeah, on a weekly basis." He laughed. "We tell lies to each other about our tours in Afghanistan. Fairy tales that begin with *this is no shit*."

"I have one more favor to ask."

"Anything, what is it?"

"Frank's going to make arrangements to have my MRAD, and a box of ammo shipped from Ft. Bragg to

Vincenza. You need to get them to his contact at Pope Field."

Mike furrowed his brow. "The three-thirty-eight magnum?"

"Yeah."

"No problem, but you think you'll need that monster over there?"

Mike grinned. "No, but I don't want to get rusty. Two or three months without practice and I wouldn't be able to hit an elephant in the ass with a one-o-five howitzer. There's a lot of open space where my family lives. With the suppressor no one will hear a thing."

"You don't lose the art we have in sixty or ninety days. Who's the Air Force guy at Pope?"

"Frank said he'll call you when they have a game plan."

"What about your appointments with the VA psychologist? What's her name?" Bob asked.

"Zoe." Mike shrugged. "I called her."

"She okay with it?"

"Yeah. Told me to continue facing the problem. Been doing it, but I don't know if that shit works."

Bob chuckled. "My guy told me I need to keep telling myself it's not real. The problem is, at the moment you see it, it's real."

"I heard the same line. Last week in the grocery store I saw a fine looking young lady in shorts and a tiny tube top. Thought I'd touch her to make sure she was really there, but I figured she'd slap me into next week."

"Might have been worth it." Bob smiled and stood. "Your guns in the car?"

"Yeah."

"Does the ammo weigh less than a hundred pounds?"

"Jesus, Bob. I'm not starting a war." Mike smiled. "Ninety pound box. I limited it to eight hundred and fifty rounds."

"Just enough for a mid-size battle. I'll send everything FedEx." Bob stood. "Let's get your guns and we'll see if Julie has lunch ready."

Once they unloaded the Jeep they walked into the kitchen. Sub sandwiches, and chips were on the table. Julie stood beside it pouring iced tea.

Everyone sat and Julie looked at Mike. "So you're not seeing wild-child Olga anymore."

Wild-child isn't half of it.

After Bob had met and married her, it became Julie's mission to fix Mike up with a woman to keep him company. She and Olga, both nurses, worked the same shift at UC Health Memorial Hospital.

"No. Not for a month or so, but it was fun while it lasted."

Julie smiled. "Was she too much for you?"

"Not really, but when she got the new roommate, I was quite surprised."

"Tatyana, the girl from St. Petersburg. I met her once. She seemed nice."

"She was. They are both wonderful young ladies, but a little hard to handle. Olga's apartment, with only one bed and bedroom, got to be somewhat crowded."

Bob laughed. "I should have such problems."

Julie smacked his arm. "You do and a black eye won't be the only bruised part on your body."

Mike realized he was going to miss Bob and Julie. He was certain she knew more about Tatyana than she told him. But that was Julie. *Help out the single guy and keep it interesting for the girls.*

Later that evening Mike left their house knowing when he returned, she'd have a new friend for him to meet. *Maybe the next one will be from Sweden.* He dropped his Jeep off at a long-term storage facility and headed to the airport where he caught a plane to Atlanta.

CHAPTER IV

THE VILLA

Mike got some sleep on the overnight flight to Leonardo da Vinci International Airport, arriving in Rome at seven.

He passed through customs without a hitch. The official looked at the Italian passport and at once identified him as a dual citizen. As soon as he spoke fluent Italian, the officer stamped it and motioned toward the exit.

###

He boarded the 9:25 flight to Reggio Calabria and arrived an hour later. After collecting the rucksack at baggage claim, he picked up a Jeep Renegade he had reserved. *They aren't expecting me.* He sat in the vehicle with the air conditioner on and dialed Pio's cell phone.

"Hi, Pio, I'm in Reggio. I rented a car and will be there by 2:30 this afternoon. How's Gina?"

"Not well... hasn't left the house except to go to the funeral." Pio paused. "I received a call. They want more money."

"I thought these guys wouldn't be back for a month." His jaw tightened. "What happened?"

"There's a lot I need to tell you. They know we can't pay that much and now want us to sign over part of the business."

"These bastards are crazy! When do we make the next payment?"

"In three days."

"Okay. You and I will sit down and figure out what must be done. Tell Gina I'll see her this afternoon."

Mike turned off the A3 Autostrada at Vibo Valentia and continued east into the hills. Barely aware of the passing countryside, he thought about what the criminals were doing to his family. They had to realize people often reinvested their profits, and couldn't afford added expenses. Then again, criminals didn't care about profits, what they get is free of any expenses. *I need to figure out what the hell I'm going to do.*

A mile past a small town, he turned onto a well maintained dirt road leading to a sprawling two-story stone villa. Four smaller buildings stood to one side of the house. He passed the side of the villa and parked beside a Mercedes and two white Fiat vans in the front yard.

He got out of the Jeep and looked at what he remembered was a large shed, now reduced to a pile of burned debris.

"Mike!" Gina shouted as she ran towards him. She leapt into his arms and kissed both his cheeks.

Mike was reminded of the cultural differences between the people back in the States and those here in Italy. Hugs and holding hands are not frowned upon among family members and friends. Handshakes were for more formal relationships. *Got to remember that.*

He held her at arms-length, wiped tears from her face, and faked a smile when he saw the bruise on her cheek. "My twenty-one-year-old cousin is as beautiful as ever."

"You forgot to add nine years." She pushed her hair over her shoulders.

"Gina, you've never looked your age. What happened to your cheek?"

"I ran into a limb in the orchard."

Mike nodded and looked at the black and blue mark. *No scuff marks from the bark.*

"How was your trip?" she asked.

"Long. It'll take a day to catch up on my sleep." He removed his suitcase, extended the handle and handed it to her. "I only have one other bag," he said as he pulled his rucksack from the vehicle.

Gina pointed at his leg and cocked her head to the side. "Why don't you take the suitcase and I'll carry that."

He slung the pack over his shoulder and took her hand. "My leg may not be pretty, but it still works."

As they walked to the house hand in hand, he stole glances at her. She had not changed since his last visit a little over a year ago. Her long black hair flowed across a white shirt and form fitting jeans were tucked into work boots. He pulled her close to his side. "I thought by now a guy would have asked this beautiful girl to marry him. Are you still waiting for Mr. Wonderful?"

Gina smiled and slapped his shoulder. "The only eligible men around here are farmers."

"Oh, I see. You're looking for a wine or olive oil executive."

She pulled his arm, and they stopped. "Do you have any good looking friends who want to marry an olive oil baroness and live in Italy?"

He kissed her on the cheek. "None of them are good enough for you."

They walked into the house and set his bags in the living room.

Gina pulled him across the room. "Pio and Rachele are in the kitchen, we'll have coffee."

"How is she? Did her son graduate from college?"

"Yes. He's a civil engineer and works in Milan. He told her she didn't need to work any longer, but she's been with us for thirty years. She loves it here."

When they stepped into the kitchen, Pio and Rachele turned.

She spotted him, squealed and jumped out of her chair.

Mike wrapped his arms around the petite sixty-year-old woman and lifted her a few inches off the ground. "The commanding general of the house. You look well." He set her down, turned to Pio and hugged him. "Sorry we had to meet again during sad times."

Pio pointed at the table and a variety of cheeses in a platter. "Sit and relax."

An hour later, Mike and Pio walked out the front door and headed to the cars.

Mike pointed at the charred wood that remained from the burned shed. "What happened?"

Pio shook his head. "They set it on fire when Romeo told them he couldn't pay what they asked. Come, we'll walk."

They strolled the well-kept dirt driveway.

"Tell me everything. Who are these men?" Mike asked.

"As I said, it started two years ago. Mafioso from Sicily began to threaten the farmers and business owners around Vibo Valentia. They demanded monthly payments, telling everyone it was for protection from criminals and unions who were planning to rob them and disrupt their businesses."

Mike furrowed his brow. "You mean the *Ndrangheta*, Calabrian organized crime, don't you?"

"No," Pio said. "The local clans lost a shipment of drugs they were moving for the Sicilians. The only way they could pay them back was to allow the Cosa Nostra family in Messina to take control in this area. To collect what they call *pizzo.*"

"Protection money." Mike stopped walking and looked at Pio. "Are we the only ones they're extorting?"

"No. Most of the large farms and businesses need to give them money every month."

Mike shook his head. "How much are the payments?"

"5,000 Euros."

"Jesus." He grabbed Pio's arm. "That's over $60,000 a year."

Pio lowered his head. "If we don't have it, they want fifty-five percent of the business."

"That isn't going to happen, Pio." Mike thought a moment. "Gina didn't hurt her face while working, did she?"

"No. It happened on the day her father was killed. She tried to help him. One of them punched her."

Mike tightened his hands into fists and felt his nails bite into both palms. "Do you know his name?"

"No, but he's usually the one that collects the money. He's short and young... maybe twenty... twenty-two. If he comes alone, he drives a Ducati motorcycle."

For the next hour they walked the long road leading to the villa and discussed the situation. Mike discovered that when the men knew they were going to be paid, they sent only one person to collect the money. If there were any questions about whether they would get paid, they sent two.

Both men were quiet on the walk back to the villa.

Pio stopped Mike outside the front door. "You can't stop them, Mike. They're like animals, they'll kill you and Gina and anyone who tries to help."

Mike placed a hand on Pio's shoulder. "For now I'll pay them, I have the money. I don't know how we'll stop them, but we'll figure out something. It'll take time, trust me. First, let's see who comes in three days. I want to talk to them."

CHAPTER V

SETTLE IN

When Mike entered the house, Gina was waiting in the living room. She grabbed his suitcase and pointed to the rucksack. "Take that, you'll stay upstairs in the large bedroom at the side of the house."

He slung the pack over his shoulder and reached for the suitcase. "I can carry both of them."

Gina placed her hands on her hips and stared at him. She pulled the carry-on to her side. "You're the one with the bad leg. I've seen it many times and unless you've had more surgery, I know what it looks like." She headed up the stairs, led him down a hallway and into a bedroom.

Mike usually stayed in a room down the hall. This one had been his father's and was later set aside for guests. He stopped and looked from left to right. *Biggest room in the house. Got to be eighteen by twenty-four.*

A queen-size bed was to his left. Lamps, made from ceramic jugs, stood on the two nightstands. On the opposite side of the room, a roll top desk was centered along a wall. A five-drawer dresser stood on each side of the desk.

He glanced at three windows in front of him. A large table, with four chairs, occupied the space in front of the center window.

He looked at Gina and raised his eyebrows. "This is the biggest bedroom I've ever seen. It must be eight meters wide and six meters deep."

"Actually it's bigger." Gina smiled. "Our grandfather used it as an office, but your dad didn't like people coming upstairs so he made it his bedroom."

Mike walked around the table and gazed at the cloudless sky out the window. From where he stood, he focused his shooter's eyes on the long winding driveway to the paved road running in front of the property. *Two hundred yards.* To the left, the paved road continued down the hillside and snaked its way toward a group of houses in the distance. *Two intersections, stop signs, and then the houses. Maybe a mile.* He turned to Gina. "I love this view," he said as he pulled out two chairs. "Sit a moment... let's talk."

Gina rolled his suitcase to the edge of the bed and walked to a chair.

He sat next to her. "Pio told me what happened to your face. The next time you see the man that did it, I want you to look at me and nod."

Her complexion turned ashen. She covered the bruise with her hand and looked away. She took a deep breath, let it out, and turned to him. "I don't want to cause problems. I shouldn't have said anything. If you confront him, it will make more trouble."

Mike nodded. "I know. You don't need to worry. I just want you to tell me which one did it."

"Okay, but please be careful."

"Pio said one of them was young, and drives a motorcycle. Was it him?"

She nodded. "Yes. He's cruel. I think he wants to impress the others."

Mike stood and held out his hand.

Gina got up, and he hugged her. "I'll have the money for them when they come, but I've got to figure out a way to stop it."

"You can't fight them, Mike."

"I won't. Give me time to decide the best way to make them leave us alone."

"I will, but I don't think they'll ever stop."

Mike grinned and kissed her cheek. "Trust me. Did you get the Italian cell phone I asked you to buy?"

"Yes." She pointed to the desk. "It's there. A G5 Android. I added names and numbers to the contact file."

"You and Pio?"

"Yes, and a few others."

"Good. Thank you. I'm going to unpack and rest for a while. I'll come downstairs later."

Gina hugged him. "Okay. We're having a big dinner tonight at eight. I invited a friend and some others that work for us who want to see you."

###

At six that evening Mike walked through the dining room on his way to the kitchen. Place settings were in front of eight chairs at the large table.

As he entered he smelled the strong fragrance of basil. Rachele stood at the kitchen counter slicing vegetables and tossing them into a strainer.

"What are we having tonight?" Whatever she made would be delicious. Every time he visited he gained weight and fought to take it off when he returned to Colorado. With his leg, running was out of the question. He reminded himself to take small portions.

"Antipasto, pasta made with fresh basil pesto, and then grilled pork and chicken," she said. "We'll have almond pudding and biscotti for dessert. To drink, we have your uncle's wine and grappa he made. Pio is bringing his homemade *Fragolino*."

Mike's eyes widened. "Wild strawberry liqueur... I love it. Where is Gina and Pio?"

"They went to check olive trees in an orchard not far from here."

He nodded. "I'll be in the living room. Call me if you need help."

After he sat, he pulled out the new cell phone and removed a small piece of paper from his wallet. He typed Frank Weatherbee's name and number into his contact file, pulled up the key pad and began a text message. "Frank, it's Mike Anello. This is my Italian cell phone number. Have you heard from Bob Keal?" He sent the message.

Ten minutes later his phone beeped, and he read Frank's response. "Yes. Will be nice to see you. Your package arrives in a few days. Let you know when I get it."

Mike answered. "Good. I'll drive up to Vicenza. See you then." He stared across the room. *I told Zoe, shooting is a form of therapy. Can't wait to start again.*

Gina walked into the room. "Did you rest?"

"Yes."

"Feeling better?"

"Much better and looking forward to one of Rachele's great meals. Who's the friend you invited? Will I like him?"

Gina tried to hide a smile. "No, but you'll like her. I told her about my handsome American cousin, and she wants to meet you."

"Did you tell her he's half-crippled?"

She frowned and pointed a finger at him. "Don't say that! I told her you were in the Army and wounded in Afghanistan."

"Sorry. It bothers me at times. I wonder what people think."

"The hell with what others think!"

He grinned. "You're right. My friends and family don't care. Tell me about this girl I'm going to meet."

"She's from Vibo. We went to college together in Naples. Her name is Adria."

"Beautiful name."

"She's very pretty. Works in Reggio."

"Doing what?"

"She teaches computer science at the University Mediterranea."

CHAPTER VI

FRIENDS

By seven thirty, Mike, Pio, Tazio, the business accountant, and Piero, the marketing manager, sat in the living room. Rachele, Gina and Pio's wife, Camilla Domi, were in the kitchen.

Preoccupied with figuring out how to stop the gangsters from extorting money from the family, Mike hadn't said much.

"You're quiet. What are you thinking?" Tazio asked.

Mike shrugged. "How much I miss this place and why I haven't spent more time here."

Pio glanced at him. "We hope you stay. There's more for you here than in America."

"My team has been increasing sales each quarter," Piero raised both hands. "Soon the Anello family will have to buy more groves."

"I thought that was what your uncle was doing when I saw how much he spent in the last year," Tazio said. "He later told me it was for private investments."

Mike looked at both men and nodded. *They don't know what's been happening.*

Pio alerted and scooted forward in his chair. "Romeo wanted to keep them secret. Now that he's gone, Mike will come up with a plan to expand."

"Me?" Mike grinned. "I have a lot to learn before I can make any suggestions."

The doorbell rang and Pio stood.

Mike heard the door creak open and saw her reflection in a mirror on the wall. *Wow!* He stood and turned. A woman walked in carrying clothes on hangers and pulling a carry-on suitcase. He froze and his mouth opened. *Gina's friend? Long auburn hair. A real beauty queen.*

"Come in Adria," Pio said. "Let me help you with your bag."

Adria smiled and pointed to a chair in the corner. "I'll put everything over there."

Mike hadn't moved. He couldn't take his eyes off her.

"Mike." Pio said.

He hesitated, still staring at Adria.

"Mike? This is Gina's friend, Adria Venere."

He closed his mouth and blinked. *Blue eyes, and olive skin!*

She walked to him and kissed his cheek. "My grandfather was from Wales," she whispered.

He smiled. *Wow, forget the Swedish girls.* "Was I that obvious?"

"Yes, with this hair and these eyes, I often get the same look. How was your trip?"

"Long, but fine. Nice to meet you. You have an advantage over me. I know little about you."

She winked at him. "We can fix that. Where's Gina?"

"Helping Rachele make dinner."

"We'll have a lot of time to talk. I'm staying for the next two days." She headed to the kitchen.

He watched her saunter to the doorway. *Yes, we will!*

Pio, grinning from ear-to-ear and moved to his side. "She's beautiful, isn't she?"

"Beautiful doesn't come close."

"I've known her father for many years. He lives in Vibo, but works as a ferryboat captain in Reggio."

"Does he have dark auburn hair and blue eyes like his daughter?"

Pio laughed. "No. His father's genes skipped a generation."

Mike rubbed his left thigh.

"Does it hurt?" Pio asked.

"A little. I think I'll go out front. Call me when dinner's ready."

He walked to the side of the house and stopped fifty feet in front of it. From where he stood he gazed across the dry, sloping landscape. He turned in a circle and surveyed the hills. *Nothing like the Middle East. Quite a few places to hide.* He walked around the corner of the house and looked up at the three windows of his second-floor bedroom. *I won't need to leave the bedroom.*

Pio called, "Mike. Come in."

###

In the dining room, he noticed the vacant chair at the head of the table. *Uncle Romeo's seat.*

Dinners at the villa were usually small unlike the afternoon meal when most chairs at the large table were filled. Romeo led the conversation and often picked out a couple of people to tease. *It won't be the same without him.*

Gina took his arm and led him to the chair. "Sit here."

Plates of sliced sausage, cold cuts, cheese and wedges of cantaloupe were passed to the men at one end of the table, and then to the women. Gina sat opposite him, ten feet away, with Adria to her right.

A five course meal filled the next three hours. Mike waited for the opportunity to spend time alone with Adria.

###

During the time Adria spent at the villa, Mike seldom left her company. They walked through the nearby olive groves and shared stories of their families and childhoods. She surprised him when she asked how he was injured, and the day his friend was killed.

She left late Sunday afternoon and within an hour he missed her beautiful face. He now realized that after retiring from the army and being released from Walter Reed Hospital, he had isolated himself. *Those days are over. Not only does Gina need my help, I'm starting to enjoy myself.*

CHAPTER VII

MEETING THE MAFIA

At seven Monday morning Mike threw on clothes and went to the kitchen.

Gina sat at a table drinking coffee.

"Good morning." He smiled. "Did you sleep well?"

"Yes, did you?"

"Like a baby." He stopped at the espresso machine, inserted the small pod, and made himself a cup. Before he walked to the table, he removed a bottle of homemade Anisette from a cabinet. When he sat, he whiffed the rich aroma of the dark coffee and noted a slight scent of chocolate. He added four drops of the sweet liquor to the cup. *A little morning kick start.*

"Did you like Adria?"

He raised his eyebrows. "Yes, and I plan to spend more time with her."

Gina winked. "I know. She's excited. She liked you too."

Mike smiled and took a sip of coffee. "I hope so. Did the twenty thousand dollars I wired to the business account come yet?"

She nodded. "Yes, Friday. It converted to a little under nineteen thousand euros."

"Good. Go to the bank today and take out five thousand in hundred euro notes. When they come tomorrow, I want them to believe there will be no problems getting their money."

Gina shook her head and took a deep breath. "What are we going to do?" Her tone was soft and uncertain. "You know this will continue each month and they may ask for more."

He reached across the table and took her hand. "Trust me, it will stop. I don't know how yet. I need more time to put everything in place."

"Put what in place?"

"That's the big question. I don't have an answer yet. After they leave tomorrow, I'm driving to Vicenza."

"That's a thousand kilometers from here. Will you be okay?" Her voice rose. "It will take two days to get there."

He squeezed her hand. "I'm not staying long. Round trip will take three days."

Gina furrowed her brow. "What's in Vicenza?"

"The American Army base. I'm meeting a friend."

"Why?"

"You're full of questions. He has a package for me. I'll explain when I get back."

"When you were in the army, everything was secret," she smiled. "I guess you'll never change."

He grinned. "More secrets. Whatever you do, tell no one where I'm going, or what I just told you."

"Okay, but be careful."

The next day, Pio, Gina, and Mike sat in the living room discussing whether they should buy more land to plant trees. The second choice would be buying established groves owned by their suppliers.

Mike wore a tan shirt, black knee-length cargo shorts and a pair of black and gray Diadora sneakers.

Gina pointed at his scarred leg and ankle. "How does it feel?"

"Not bad. Looks like hell, but I'll live."

The sound of a car pulling up to the house interrupted them.

Pio walked to the window. "They're here. Two of them. The young guy is the one who hit Gina."

Mike picked up a thick envelope and stood. "I don't want them in the house." He strode to the door and stopped. "Remember, don't be confrontational. We want them to think we've given up and are going along with their agenda."

"Are you sure?" Gina asked.

"Yes. Let me do the talking."

Mike exaggerated his limp as the three of them walked to the front yard.

Two men got out of an old Fiat.

Mike stopped in front of them. "I'm Mike Anello, one of the owners of Casa Anello Olive Oil." He did not extend his hand.

Both men wore matching work shirts stained with what looked like oil and grease. The name *Antonio Garage* was embroidered on their left breast pocket.

They stared at his scars. The older, taller man spoke. "My name is Sisto, and this is Enzo." He pointed. "What happened to your leg?"

"Motorcycle accident."

"A Ducati?" Enzo asked.

So this little asshole is the one who hits women. "No, a Harley Davidson. My riding, running, and sometimes walking days have ended."

Both men avoided looking at the leg.

"Do you have our money?" Enzo asked.

Mike glanced at him. A leather shoulder bag hung at his side, the strap crossing his chest. "Yes, five thousand." He handed Sisto the thick envelope.

Sisto passed it to Enzo, who put it in the bag. "Good. Enzo will return in a month for the next payment... another five thousand."

"There will be no problems. You'll get your money. I don't want my family or workers threatened again."

Sisto stared at him. "That depends on you. Do what we ask, and make sure we get paid."

Mike nodded. "You will."

The two men got into the car and drove away.

Back in the house, Mike, Gina, and Pio sat at the kitchen table. Rachele made coffee and left.

Mike looked at Pio. "Tell me about *Antonio Garage*."

"It's outside of town... not far from here. A year ago, the owner, Pasquale Juliano, couldn't pay. They forced him and his son to sign the business over to them. The old man later killed himself."

Mike shook his head. "That will not happen to us. From now on, we need to keep our conversations to ourselves. Don't share what we say with anyone. I'm leaving for Vicenza this evening. When I return, the three of us need to sit and talk," He glanced at them. "And again, don't tell anyone I drove to Vicenza."

Pio shifted in his seat. "Don't you want to explain what you're planning?"

"If I knew, I would. My trip is nothing more than to pick up something to keep me busy." He handed Gina three hundred euros. "While I'm gone, buy a stereo and set it up in my bedroom."

Gina looked at the bills. "This is too much!"

He smiled. "I don't want a cheap system. I want to hear and feel the music."

CHAPTER VIII

THE SET UP

It took Mike thirteen hours to drive to Camp Del Din, the home of the 173rd Airborne Brigade Combat Team in Vicenza. He had never been to the new base which opened in 2013. Frank Weatherbee, the armorer for the second battalion, had given him directions to his office.

He turned right, into a parking lot. The building and door Frank described, with paratrooper wings imposed over crossed rifles, stood thirty feet in front of him.

As he walked in, a sergeant sitting at a desk to his right looked at him. "Can I help you, sir?"

"Yeah. I'm Sergeant First Class Mike Anello. I'm here to see Frank Weatherbee."

The sergeant stood and extended his hand. "He told me to expect you." He pointed down a hallway. "Second door on the left."

Mike looked at the name on the man's uniform and smiled. "Major. I'll bet that name gets you in trouble at times."

The sergeant laughed. "When I arrived here, the Battalion Sergeant Major reminded me he was the only Sergeant Major in the unit. For the first month it got so bad I thought about changing my name to Smith."

Mike grinned. "I once worked for a major whose last name was Minor... Major Minor." He headed to the hall.

Frank must have heard Mike's voice and came out of his office. "Well. The man with the golden scope. You still getting those first round hits?"

They shook hands, and Frank pulled him in the office and closed the door.

"Have a seat," Frank said. "How's the olive oil business? That why you're in Italy?"

"Yeah, and sales are good."

Frank shook his head. "When you were on active duty, you were the only guy in the army who made three times more on the side than his army pay."

"Actually it was four times. It's called ownership."

Frank raised his hand. "I'm doing my part. My wife buys your oil at a market downtown... couldn't find it online."

"I think that may be my next move. Just need to find the right person to set up the site and promote it." He paused. "My stuff get here in one piece?"

Frank stepped to a metal cabinet against the wall and pulled open the double doors. "Everything you asked Bob to send."

A six-foot long cardboard carton stood against the side of the cabinet. A heavily taped box sat at the bottom.

"Any hitches?" Mike asked.

"No. Came with two pallets of new parachutes from Ft. Bragg."

Mike looked at the big box and squinted. "What's stenciled on it?"

"Definitely not Mike Anello's sniper rifle". He chuckled. "Shelves, metal, gray, ten each. The small one says bolts, nuts, washers, one hundred pounds. You plan to take this back south?"

"Yeah. We're out in the country... lots of open space. I'd go nuts if I couldn't practice."

Frank raised his eyebrows. "Whatever you do, don't let the Italian cops see it. They're not big fans of widow-makers owned by olive farmers."

Mike stood. "Come on, I'll take you to lunch... then I need to get on the road."

At two-thirty in the afternoon, Mike turned onto the A-13 Autostrada and headed toward Bologna. He opened the center console, removed a prescription bottle and downed a single pill. *No hotel tonight.*

Hours later, on a dark section of the A-3 south of Rome, he noticed blue lights and flashing headlights in his rearview mirror. He glanced at his speedometer, *seventy-five,* and eased his foot from the accelerator. "Damn, I'm not going that fast."

The police lights were rapidly closing on the Jeep *How am I going to bullshit my way out of this one? If they ask what's in the big box, I'm finished.* He stayed in the right lane and held his breath.

As he watched the police car approach, his eyes widened. "That guy's flying!"

Ten seconds later a light blue and white striped Lamborghini flew past him. He had only a second to make out *Polizia* painted on the side. "Jesus! He's going at least a hundred and fifty."

###

Mike parked his Jeep outside the villa at seven-thirty the next morning.

Gina ran from the house. "I can't believe you're back. Where did you stay?"

"I didn't. I haven't been to bed for over forty hours."

She rubbed the stubble on his cheek. "I can tell. You're in the same clothes you were wearing when you left."

He slid the long box from the Jeep. "Can you take this to my bedroom? I'll get the other one, it's heavier."

"Yes." She picked up the box. "You better go to bed. I'll tell everyone to be quiet."

Mike lifted a box from the back seat and placed it on his right shoulder.

When they walked into his bedroom, he pointed at the table in front of the window. "Put it there." He set the small, heavy carton on the floor.

Gina cocked her head, put the box on the table and placed a hand on it. "What's in here?"

"I'll show you later. Right now, I'm beat and need to rest."

"What time do you want me to wake you?"

"You don't need to, I'll set my alarm for three," Mike said. "Can you call Pio and tell him to be here at four? I want to talk to both of you."

"I will. I'll tell Rachele to have something for you to eat at a little after three." She left the room.

He looked at the two boxes and took a deep breath. *They can wait.* He stripped off his wrinkled clothes and fell into bed.

Mike woke at three, showered, and twenty minutes later headed downstairs. Even before he walked into the kitchen, he caught the sweet smell of garlic sautéing.

Rachele stood over a pot of steaming water and a sizzling frying pan. Beside her, a raw steak lay on a plate. "Are you hungry?"

"I'm starving. You're an angel for making me something in the middle of the day." He inserted a pod in the espresso machine, placed a cup under the spout, and pressed the button.

"No one goes hungry in this house," Rachele said. "How do you want your steak cooked?"

He glanced at the thickness of the meat and the hot cast iron frying pan on the stove. "Four minutes on each side... medium rare."

Rachele smiled. "So did Romeo."

The mention of his uncle's name saddened him. He placed an arm around Rachele's waist. "I miss him."

She patted his hand. "He's here watching over us."

Mike sat at the table and filled his glass from a bottle of San Pellegrino.

Rachele placed a plate of pasta with mushrooms, cherry tomatoes, and baby asparagus in front of him. "By the time you finish that, the steak will be ready." She put an empty glass and a bottle of homemade wine in front of him. "After the steak I have cucumbers and escarole in olive oil and lemon juice."

"You're going to make me fat."

"No, strong."

Gina and Pio walked into the room.

Rachele pointed at the table. "Sit, I'll make coffee."

Gina kissed Mike's cheek. "Feeling better?"

"Yes, much."

Rachele placed two cups, sugar and spoons on the table. "As soon as I finish the steak, I'm going home. I'll be back at seven-thirty in the morning."

While he ate, Gina and Pio drank their coffee and remained silent until Rachele departed.

Gina stared at Mike before she spoke. "Are you going to tell us what you've been keeping secret?"

Pio glanced at Gina, furrowed his brow and turned to Mike. "Have you thought about what we're going to do?"

Mike smiled. "It's been on my mind constantly, but I haven't come up with a plan yet. Most of them are cowards and prey on people because it's easy. If someone makes it difficult for them, they'll quit."

Pio shook his head. "It may not be that easy. These bastards know people are frightened and will pay because they don't have a way to stop them."

"Mike, I don't understand," Gina said. "Nothing will frighten them."

"Everyone is afraid of something." He shrugged. "With luck, I'll figure out what they fear. Right now, my top priority is to relax and spend time enjoying myself. I want to show you something, let's go upstairs."

###

When they reached his bedroom door he stopped. "This could get me in trouble with the authorities. My future is in your hands."

"Your secret is safe with us," Pio said. "This is the south. The family is first, followed by the business, the local soccer team, the church, and our friends. Somewhere near the bottom of the list is the local commune, and the State."

Gina wagged a finger at him. "Mike, there's nothing that could make us hurt or endanger you."

Mike opened the door, and they followed him to the table in front of the open window.

Before he had gone downstairs, he unpacked and assembled his sniper rifle. He screwed the Bushnell range finder onto a twelve inch high tripod and set it near the stock of the weapon. He had covered everything with a blanket.

Mike uncovered the rifle.

Gina gasped and put her hand over her mouth. Pio froze. Their wide eyes locked on the five foot long weapon.

As she stared, she placed her hand over her heart. "My God! Where did you get that?"

"I bought it last year... picked it up when I went to Vicenza."

Gina glanced at the open rifle case under the table. "That's what was in the big box?"

"Yes. Do you want me to send it back to America?"

Gina turned a questioning look to him. "No, but tell me why you brought it here."

"I enjoy shooting... it helps me relax. The psychologist at the veteran's hospital told me I had to confront my problem with flashbacks of the war. She suggested I shoot as often as possible. It's a form of therapy."

A wide grin lit up Pio's face.

"What are you thinking?" Mike asked.

Pio looked at Gina and raised his eyebrows. "Excuse me, Gina." He turned to Mike. "You have a big set of balls. I love it!"

"So, you're both okay with this?" Mike asked. "There may be problems if the police find it here."

"Neither of us are concerned," Pio said.

Gina nodded.

Mike walked to the open window and motioned to them. "Come here. To the left. Do you see the three stop signs along the road going toward town?"

Pio nodded.

"Yes," Gina said. "But the ones the farthest away are hard to see."

"Okay." Mike moved back around the table and looked through the range finder. "Look through this, but don't move it."

Gina leaned forward. "Oh. Yes, I see it. What are the numbers?"

"Distance to the sign in meters and other information I need to make an accurate shot."

Gina looked again. "It says nine hundred and fifty-two! You can shoot that sign?"

"Yes, but that one is a little far." He lifted a piece of paper from the table and scanned his notes. "The first sign is four hundred and sixty-six meters, the second is five hundred and eleven. Those two are much easier to hit, but I don't want to use them for target practice. If I decide to shoot from here, I'll aim at jugs of water."

Pio stepped to the table and looked through the range finder. "Amazing."

Mike tapped him on the shoulder and pointed out the window. "There's a stone wall near the second stop sign. Tomorrow morning I want you to put a plastic liter jug full of water at the base of the wall. Place it near the end closest to the street. When you arrive here, we'll come to my room and I'll shoot it." He pointed at the rifle. "You need to see what this baby can do."

Gina frowned. "You can't do that. Someone will report the sound of a gunshot."

"No one will hear it." Mike tapped the suppressor. "This eliminates most of the sound. You'll see in the morning." He motioned to the table. "One more thing. I need a place to put all this."

"Just cover it with the blanket," Gina said.

He raised his eyebrows. "No. If anyone sees it, your cousin will be in the Vibo Valentia jail."

Pio looked at Gina with wide eyes and lifted both of his hands, palms raised.

She walked to the dresser on the left side of the desk, kneeled, and removed the empty bottom drawer.

"It won't fit in there," Mike said.

She leaned over and reached inside the opening.

Mike heard a click.

She stood and grabbed the right side of the dresser. "Put it in here." She swung the bureau away from the wall.

Mike's jaw dropped, and he stared at an opening. "It's a room?"

Gina shook her head. "No. It's a space one and a half meters deep, but it runs the length of the wall. The light switch is to the right."

Mike closed his mouth, took a deep breath and exhaled. "Wow. What's in there?"

Gina paused. "Pio will explain everything better than I can."

Pio smiled. "During the war, our grandfathers fought side-by-side in the resistance."

"World War II?"

"Yes. They built this space to hide stuff from the Germans. They never destroyed the guns they used. A few of them are still wrapped in cloth inside there."

"Pio and I are the only ones that know of this." Gina headed to the door. "I better go downstairs in case someone comes."

"How many guns?" Mike asked Pio.

"Ten."

"Holy shit! Rifles?"

Pio grinned. "Two shotguns, four German rifles, and four pistols."

"Christ! Is that all?"

"Yes. When your uncle and I were young men, we threw the grenades into the sea."

Mike's jaw dropped for the second time. "Grenades?"

Pio nodded.

Mike shook his head. "Thank God. Seventy-five-year-old grenades would be incredibility unstable." He headed to the opening. "Let's take a peek."

For the next hour Mike and Pio examined the shotguns, two German K-98 bolt action rifles, and two MP-40 submachine guns. They unwrapped a pair of Walther P-38 pistols, and two Luger P-08 pistols. A large crate of ammunition sat in a corner.

Mike turned to Pio. "And I was dumb enough to think you and Gina were upset when you saw my rifle." He picked up a MP-40. "I have an idea. Do you know anyone who owns a machine shop with good size drills and a lathe?"

"Yes."

"Do you think he'll let me use the equipment to make something?"

Pio grinned. "One of the owners will. You'll need to ask the other one when we go downstairs."

Mike furrowed his brow. "Downstairs?"

"I own twenty-five percent of the shop and Gina now owns seventy-five. The Anello family oil business pays the

Anello family machine shop to keep all their equipment running."

CHAPTER IX

THE GAMES START

After spending the evening with Pio and Gina, Mike went to bed, still tired from the drive to Vicenza. He woke in the middle of the night when he landed on the floor beside the bed. "Dave! Keep your head down!" he screamed.

As he jumped up and raced downstairs, he wiped the side of his head and looked at his bloody hand. He bolted through the front door and stopped in front of the villa.

Suddenly, reality came back into focus, and he realized he stood near the villa in Italy, and not on the outskirts of a village in Afghanistan. He raised both hands. No blood or brain matter covered his skin. *Friggin nightmares.*

"Mike! Are you okay?" Gina called from the front porch.

He spun toward the voice and relaxed when he saw his cousin in her pajamas. "Yes. I'm fine."

She pointed at his underwear. "Go put on your pants and come to the kitchen."

A few minutes later he walked into the kitchen wearing a pair of cargo shorts. He wet a dishtowel and wiped sweat from his neck and arms.

"I heard you yell, and you weren't in your room. It's still happening, isn't it?" Gina asked.

He nodded. "But not as often."

She made two cups of coffee and they sat at the table. "I worry about you."

He leaned toward her and smiled. "I know. Everything is all right. After a few seconds I knew it wasn't real."

"Is there something I can do to help?"

"Yes." He sat erect, snapped his shoulders back, and grinned. "Invite your friend, Adria, more often."

Gina laughed and downed her espresso. "You like her, don't you?"

"I enjoyed every minute with her."

"I'll call her today."

Gina made them an early breakfast, and they spent the next few hours discussing the business and his ideas to expand sales.

Later that morning, Mike heard the door open and Pio walked into the living room.

"Good morning," Pio said. "I set the jug of water beside the road."

Mike stood and pointed at a leather case in Pio's hand. "Did you bring the binoculars?"

"Yes."

"Good. Get Gina and come upstairs."

In his room, Mike opened the window, and pushed the table against the wall. He positioned his rifle, so it pointed out the window and placed the range finder and a single .338 bullet next to it. He walked to the stereo Gina had purchased and loaded a disc.

Gina and Pio came in and closed the door.

Mike motioned them to the table. "I already made the adjustments on the scope." He placed a second chair to the right of the rifle. "Gina, you sit here and watch through that," he said pointing at the range finder. "Pio, stand behind me with your binoculars."

Gina sat and looked at the jug, five hundred meters from the villa. She turned to Mike. "It's so small. I don't see how you're going to hit it."

He placed a hand on her shoulder. "Trust me, I will. The bullet will take under a half second to travel to the target, so don't blink. You ready?"

She nodded.

Mike walked to the stereo and pressed a button. Rod Stewart's *Rhythm of my Heart* began to play, and he turned up the volume. He sat beside Gina, and Pio stepped behind him.

"Why the music?" she asked.

"It helps me control my heartbeat."

"Will the gunshot be loud?" Pio asked.

"No louder than the music. But Gina, if you want, put your hands over your ears."

He slid the bullet into the chamber, closed the bolt and raised the stock. Pressing it against his shoulder, he positioned his right eye inches from the scope, took a deep breath and slowly exhaled. For the next few seconds he slowed his breathing and began to exert pressure on the trigger during the pause between breaths.

The dull crack of the rifle made Gina jump. She shoved her chair away from the table and looked at him, her eyes the size of golf balls. "The jug exploded!"

"Not really. The bullet travels so fast, it looked that way." He ejected the shell casing, stood and looked at Pio. "Good therapy, isn't it?"

He nodded. "With the music playing, the only sound was a pop."

###

For the next three days, Mike and Pio spent most of their evenings at R&P Metal Fabrication in Vibo Valentia. They made two eight inch long suppressors out of high grade stainless steel. Once finished, they machined threads into the barrels of the MP-40 submachine guns so the suppressors could be attached.

When their work at the machine shop ended, they returned to the villa, went to Mike's bedroom, and pulled the dresser from the wall.

Once inside the narrow chamber, they reassembled the submachine guns and loaded one magazine with thirty rounds of nine millimeter ammunition.

"Is the truck ready?" Mike asked.

"Yes."

Mike inserted the magazine into one of the guns, and they returned to his room where he set it on the table. "Tell me what the front of *Antonio Garage* looks like."

Pio smiled. "Easy target. It's on a large lot near the A3 highway."

"What about other buildings?"

"It's the only structure. Two service doors and retail space with an office on one side. The front of the store has large windows with the business name painted on them."

Mike nodded. "How far is the building from the street?"

Pio shrugged. "Maybe twenty meters."

"Good, we'll leave at midnight. The Mafia needs to know if our business isn't safe, neither is theirs."

Mike sat in the passenger side seat as Pio drove the one-ton flatbed truck onto a road paralleling the A3 highway.

"One kilometer on the right." Pio said. "There are lights above the doors."

"Just before we reach it, speed-up. Let me know when we're close." Mike pulled back the bolt of the MP-40. "I hate these blow back pieces of shit. One big bump, and the bolt will fly forward and fire one round."

Minutes later, Pio took his foot off the gas and down-shifted. "Fifty meters."

Mike turned in his seat and raised the submachine gun. He didn't dare rest the suppressor on the window frame for fear the vibration of the truck would release the bolt.

Pio pressed the gas pedal. The truck rumbled as it increased speed.

As they passed the front of the garage, Mike pulled the trigger. In four seconds, the bolt of the MP-40 slammed back and forth, emptying the magazine as thirty 9mm rounds shattered the two large windows. He lowered the weapon and yelled, "Let's get the hell out of here!"

The next morning, Mike sat with Pio at the kitchen table while Rachele served bread, marmalade, cheese and coffee. Both men had smiles on their faces when Gina walked into the room.

"Good morning." She sat and glanced at them. "Why the smiles?"

Mike froze. *Think of something, quick.*

"We went for a few drinks last night," Pio said.

"And that's funny?"

"Yes, Mike's not a Grappa drinker."

Gina shook a finger at Mike. "That stuff is dangerous if you're not used to it." She grinned. "Adria is coming this afternoon. Think you can put up with her for a while? She doesn't need to leave until Sunday."

Mike laughed. "I'll try."

Pio leaned toward him. "Have her take you to Pizzo. There's a couple of good restaurants along the shoreline at the base of the cliffs."

CHAPTER X

THE MEETING

When Adria arrived Mike couldn't take his eyes off her. She wore tan stiletto heels, peach leggings and a long cream blouse decorated with prints of ancient Greek ruins. Her long auburn hair hung over her right shoulder. *Wow, they dress nice over here. Even more beautiful than I remembered.*

Two hours after she arrived, they drove to La Ruota restaurant at the Pizzo Marina.

She chose one of the tables farthest from the door. "Outside the view of the marina is pretty at night."

Mike pulled out a chair. "You've been here before so you can choose what we'll order tonight. The one thing I do want is a bottle of good red wine."

The waiter strolled to the table. "Good evening. I'm Nunzio. Welcome to La Ruota. Would you like something to drink?"

Adria nodded. "Yes. A bottle of Tramonti Rosso. We'll order an antipasto when you return."

The waiter nodded and left.

A woman walked out of the restaurant and stopped beside them. "Hi Adria, who is your friend?" She kissed Adria's cheek.

"Mike Anello."

"The Anello olive oil family?"

"Yes, Gina's cousin from America. Mike, this is Bianca, the owner of La Ruota."

He stood. "Nice to meet you. Adria said you have the best restaurant in Pizzo."

"It is. The fish we serve is fresh-caught daily."

They both sat and Bianca placed a hand on Mike's arm. "I'm sorry to hear of Romeo's death. I attended the funeral. Was he—"

"My father's brother," Mike said.

She shook her head. "My condolences."

"Thank you."

"How long will you be visiting?"

"As long as my cousin needs help."

"Good, then we'll see each other again." Bianca stood. "Enjoy your meal." She leaned to Adria and smiled. "Don't order the octopus, it's a day old."

For the next two and a half hours Mike focused on finding out more about Adria as they enjoyed an antipasto, a first plate of pasta and clams in a white wine sauce, and a second plate of fish.

When they had finished dinner, Mike ordered Limoncello.

Over the past few days he considered his plan to expand Casa Anello Olive Oil. *She'll be the perfect fit.* "How do you like your job at the university?"

Adria shrugged. "It's good, but I wish it was closer to home. The apartment in Reggio is expensive."

"Would you move back to Vibo if you could find a job that pays more?"

"A job in Vibo?" She laughed. "There aren't any around here that pay enough."

"What if there was? Let's say fifty percent more a month."

She raised her eyebrows. "Of course, but that will never happen. Farmers and business that cater to tourists can't afford to pay as much as they do in Reggio."

"The position has nothing to do with tourists. It's for someone with advanced computer skills." Mike grinned. "Gina told me you're a computer and Internet expert."

She lifted her shot glass, sipped the sweet lemon liqueur, and smiled. "Expert? I don't know, but I do teach Web Design, Network Systems and Marketing. How did you hear about a job around here? You just arrived."

Mike reached across the table and took her hand. "I'm the one who is creating the position. I want to make Casa Anello a global business... sell our oil online. I'm looking for a Director of Online Sales. Someone to set up the website, make sure it looks professional and figure out what to do to make all that happen. You interested?"

"Yes! But I need to learn more before I commit to such a move."

"Good. When we get back to the villa we'll talk with Gina."

Enzo walked past their table without looking at them. Mike noticed Adria's lips press together as she frowned. Out of the corner of his eye, he watched him take a seat at a small table near the door. He leaned toward her. "Don't turn and look. You reacted when you saw the man that walked past us. Do you know him?"

Adria took a deep breath. 'I know of him. He's from Sicily. His name is Enzo."

Mike nodded. "You know about the extortion money people must pay him and his friends?"

"Yes, most people know." Adria leaned across the table and lowered her voice. "Who told you?"

"No one. I met him, and a man named Sisto. Like many other business owners, I had to pay them what they demanded."

"He's dangerous, Mike... a Mafioso from Messina." She reached out and clamped her fingers around his wrist.

He glanced at her hand. *She's shaking.*

"Even members of the local Ndrangheta clans are afraid of him and his Sicilian friends," she whispered.

"I think I'll play with his mind." He looked up, caught Enzo's eye, and nodded. Mike raised his arm to signal the waiter. "Send the little man sitting alone near the door another beer. Tell him it's from his friend," he added.

The waiter leaned to him. "Are you sure?" he whispered.

Adria's right. He's worried... everyone's scared. "Yes, put it on my bill."

The waiter nodded and headed into the restaurant.

Adria shifted in her chair. Her gaze darted to Enzo and then back to Mike. "What are you doing?"

"Being friendly."

She finished her Limoncello. "I'm scared. Let's go back to the house."

Mike paid the bill. "Everything will be okay." He took her hand and led her from the restaurant.

As he neared his Jeep, Mike heard footsteps. He turned and saw Enzo approaching with a beer in his hand.

He thrust the bottle at Mike. "You can't buy me. I get what I want. When I come to collect, add another five hundred Euros."

Adria moved to Mike's side.

Mike pulled her close and stepped between her and Enzo. "So, you're stealing money from your boss. He won't be happy if he discovers you're only thinking of yourself."

Enzo glared at him. "I suggest you don't tell him, or you'll be limping on both legs." He turned and walked away.

You're not talking to Snow White, asshole.

Later that evening, Mike, Adria, and Gina discussed the incident with Enzo as they drank coffee at the kitchen table.

"I couldn't believe Mike sent him a beer," Adria said.

He shrugged. "It's going to cost me five hundred Euros, but it's worth it."

Gina raised her eyebrows. "How? We can't afford it."

"Now he thinks I'm scared of him."

Adria turned to him and paused. "Aren't you?"

"No. Soon the Calabrian thugs will get tired of these Sicilians. Pio told me many of the business owners are complaining to the clan leaders." Mike steepled his fingers and glanced at the women. "I don't think the local gangs will put up with them much longer."

"I hope they won't. Let's change the subject." Gina said. She looked at Adria. "What do you think of the job proposal Mike made?"

Mike felt his muscles relax. He did not want to continue discussing Enzo, the Ndrangheta, or the Mafia and their extortion racket in front of Adria. *This is about family.* If she pressed him for more information, he'd skirt the subject.

A loud crack, and the sound of glass shattering, brought everyone to their feet.

A gunshot! Mike raised his hand. "Stay here!"

"Mike!" Gina yelled as he dashed from the kitchen.

He stopped at a broken glass side panel next to the front door and then ran outside. In the distance, taillights sped along the road in front of the villa.

Knowing the danger had passed, he trotted back into the house. "Gina! Adria! It's okay now."

Both women rushed into the room, their faces pale.

Gina stared at the broken glass on the floor and grabbed his arm. "What happened?"

Adria stood frozen with her hand over her mouth.

Mike scanned the wall across from the door and spotted a hole. He pointed. "We know what made that. Someone is trying to scare us."

Both women stared at the small hole.

"That's a bullet hole? Gina asked.

Mike nodded.

"It worked, they don't need to try hard to scare me," Adria said. Her cell phone rang. Before she looked at it, she turned to Mike with wide eyes.

"Who is it?" he asked.

She glanced at the screen and relaxed. "My mother is calling." She headed into the kitchen.

Gina moved beside Mike and whispered. "What are we going to do?"

"Nothing yet, but I'm getting angry." Mike feared for his cousin's safety. He and Pio had agreed they would no longer let the Mafia steal their money or their property. Neither man wanted Gina to be a part of anything they did. He took her hands. "You're worried what may happen next, aren't you?"

A tear rolled down her cheek. She wiped it and twisted her necklace chain. "Yes."

"Don't. Pio and I will handle it."

Adria walked back into the room.

"Is everything okay?" Gina asked.

"Yes. What about you?"

Gina took a deep breath and nodded. "I'm frightened, but they'll never know it."

"Good. My mother needs me to take her to Reggio in the morning. She's meeting my father when his ferry arrives. He sprained his ankle and doesn't think he can drive home. I'll take time off work and come back to discuss the job. Will you two be okay?"

Mike pulled his keys from his pocket. "No problem. Do you want me to follow you to her house?"

"No. I'll be fine. Stay here with Gina."

CHAPTER XI

PRESSURE AND RETALIATION

Gina, shaken up by the day's events, went to bed early. Mike called Pio and told him to come to the villa.

A little after midnight, he and Pio walked to the Jeep. Mike, dressed in black pants and a black shirt, carried his army rucksack and the partially disassembled sniper rifle wrapped in a dark brown blanket. He handed the keys to Pio. "You drive and drop me off at the spot you told me about."

Pio slid behind the wheel and pulled onto the dirt road leading from the house. "It's half a kilometer from the garage."

"Okay. Leave the area after I get out. Come back in fifty minutes."

###

A half hour later, Mike got out of the Jeep and eased the door closed. When Pio drove away, he crouch-ran to a clump of trees. He glanced at his watch and continued through brush and trees until he reached the top of a hill and saw the lights of *Antonio Garage*.

Mike knelt in a thicket across the two-lane road in front of the building. Once he unwrapped and assembled the rifle, he laid it on a blanket beside his backpack. He removed the rangefinder from his pack and examined the structure. *Elevation is fifteen meters... one hundred and five meters to the front door.* Mike panned to the left and then back to the right where he spotted two men under a light at the corner of the garage. Both held shotguns.

After Mike laid on the blanket, he raised the stock to his shoulder and chambered a round. It took him little time to focus on the men and adjust his scope.

For the next few minutes he watched the men talking. *Shoulder to shoulder. Let's see them start dancing.* Lowering his aim, he picked a spot on the concrete two meters in front of one of the guards.

Mike had told Pio what he would do. The two men, probably Mafia associates, were nothing more than hired hands. Killing them would be easy, but then they wouldn't be around to talk about what happened. He chuckled to himself. *Stories create fear.* As he exerted pressure on the trigger, the words from Rod Stewart's song *Some Guys Have All the Luck,* popped into his mind.

A microsecond after a puff of dust appeared on the cement, one man jumped into the air and landed on his ass.

Mike chambered another round and fired. The second guard dropped beside his partner. Both grabbed their feet and ankles.

Mike bit his lip to keep from laughing when he heard their agonizing screams. He chambered another bullet and fired at a spot on the ground to the left of the men. His next shot hit a half meter to their right.

He pushed himself to his knees, disassembled the rifle, and wrapped it in the blanket. He slung the rucksack over his shoulder and backed into the tree line.

When he reached the spot where Pio had dropped him off, he kneeled and looked at his watch. *Forty-five minutes... not bad.*

Pio arrived on time. He slid into the Jeep, and they started back to the villa.

"Did the cuts you put in the bullets work the way you said they would?" Pio asked.

"Perfectly. When the first two bullets hit the cement, they broke into small pieces that ricocheted a few inches above the ground. Both guys tap danced for a couple of seconds and then went down. The next two shots had them scooting left and right on their asses. I didn't wait around to see if they pissed their pants."

Pio laughed. "I would have loved to see it. You think they'll realize the bullets intentionally missed?"

Mike shrugged. "Doesn't matter. They'll wonder if someone is a bad shot, or could have killed them but didn't. Either way, when they tell the story it will scare the shit out of people."

"And their bandaged feet will add to the tale."

"A week in wheelchairs will do them well."

"So, we're terrorists?" Pio asked.

"That's a tough question to answer. One man's terrorist is another man's freedom fighter. Some say that quote is attributed to Yasser Arafat, but I don't think he's the first one who said it."

Pio nodded. "Maybe not, but it's true."

"Think about the Italian Financial Police and the American Internal Revenue Service. They come to your house and tell you to pay your taxes or go to jail. Is that terrorism?"

Pio laughed. "It terrorizes the hell out of me."

"Look at our grandfathers. They fought in the resistance against the Nazis. Were they terrorists?"

"No. Let's just call what we're doing a form of strong persuasion."

Mike grinned and slapped the dashboard. "Sounds good to me. We're activists trying to convince a bad company to quit charging for a service that isn't real."

"The problem is the company president doesn't listen well."

"He will, Pio. I'm not sure how yet, but he will."

CHAPTER XII

BORTOLO UMBRO

Bortolo Umbro, the man called The Spark Plug on the streets, sat at a table in the shadows of *Lo Spirito* bar in Messina. He brushed a piece of lint off his black silk shirt. *Who has the balls to shoot at my men?* Two large goons occupied a table in front of him. Both faced the front of the bar.

He grabbed an open bottle of wine. As he filled his glass, a small amount spilled onto the table. The puddle of red liquid further irritated him. Nothing had gone as planned for the last few days.

Bortolo looked up when Sisto stepped in and froze two feet from the table. *Now I'll get some answers,* he thought as he pointed at a chair.

Sisto eased down, folded his hands on his lap and stared at them. "Good evening, sir."

The Mafia boss slid a glass to him and pointed to the wine bottle.

"Thank you." Sisto half-filled it.

He stared at Sisto for five seconds before he spoke. "Is something wrong with my wine?"

"No, sir. Sorry." He snatched up the glass and took a gulp. "It's very good."

Bortolo rubbed his goatee. "I hear business has slowed at the garage."

"Yes... but we're... we're almost done making repairs and replacing the merchandise that was destroyed," he said stumbling over his words.

"Good, make it quick. We need to keep money flowing through there. Dirty Euros are difficult to spend. Tell me what happened."

Sisto took a deep breath and downed more wine. He reached for the bottle, stopped, and looked at the boss.

Bortolo pushed the bottle to him.

"Both men were shot in their feet. Whoever did it wasn't good with a gun. Two of the bullets missed."

"Do you think it was one of the Calabrian clans?"

Sisto furrowed his brow. "No. I asked. They wouldn't dare do anything like that."

"They wouldn't? We're stealing their fucking money. You better hope they never find out we hijacked our own drug shipment." He moved the wine bottle, leaned across the table and glared. "I want to know who is crazy enough to shoot our men. Start putting pressure on every asshole we're dealing with. I want answers soon." He tapped the table. "How is my nephew?"

"Enzo's a good worker, but he doesn't think we're paying him enough."

Bortolo smiled. "He's still young. Are you giving him five percent?"

"Yes."

"Good. Tell him I said he needs to learn the business before he makes demands. And make sure he doesn't get hurt. My sister will kill me."

"Sir, sometimes he opens his mouth when he should keep it shut."

"So does everyone else in my family." Bortolo raised a finger and wagged it. "Keep him away from the local clan members. I don't want any problems."

"I will."

"The last time I saw him, he told me you met an American who said he owns Casa Anello."

"We did." Sisto nodded. "He got there after we took care of the old man."

"Tell me about him. Will he become a problem for us?"

"No. He's a cripple."

Bortolo furrowed his brow. "Crippled? How?"

"We saw his leg when we met him." Sisto shuddered. "It's covered with large scars from a motorcycle accident. Ugly looking. He limps."

Bortolo focused on the wine bottle. He tapped his knuckles on the table. "I want that damn olive oil business. Before we run it into the ground, we can put one or two million Euros through it. Did you tell the American we want another payment because of what happened at the garage?"

Sisto shook his head. "No. Enzo talked to a man named Pio. He's the manager. He said he'll have the money tomorrow."

"And the others?"

"Enzo will get envelops from nine people. They are complaining but can do nothing."

"Good. Work on finding out who did the shooting. You might need to put off collecting for a few days. And tell the clan bosses the fee will increase if they don't help us."

"I will."

Bortolo raised a finger. "One more thing. Remind my nephew he is to take only five percent for himself."

CHAPTER XIII

LITTLE CAESAR

The next day, Mike and Rachele were talking when Pio walked into the kitchen.

Pio held his cell phone and waved it. "That guy Sisto called."

Mike shook his head. "What the hell does he want?"

"He said he'll be here in a few minutes. In a couple of days they're going to be collecting another payment because of the shooting at the garage, but now he wants to talk to you and me."

Mike took a seat, and Pio joined him. "About what?"

"He didn't say, but he was friendly. And that bothers me."

"Maybe they're worried." He tilted his head toward Rachele, standing at the stove, and raised his eyebrows. "Didn't you say someone shot two men standing outside

Antonio Garage? They may want to know if we heard any rumors."

Pio smiled and nodded. "I only heard what the people in town told me."

Mike shoved his chair back. "Let's meet them out front. I don't ever want them to set foot into this house."

He and Pio walked to the front porch and sat in chairs near the door.

"I'm going to tell them we can't pay," Mike said. "I want to see their reaction."

"Be careful. That's what your uncle did. Two days later, they killed him."

"I'm mad as hell, but I'll watch what I say." He turned his head toward the sound of an approaching car. "The same old Fiat, that's them."

They watched the car pull up the driveway and stop in front of the house. Sisto and Enzo got out.

Mike exaggerated his limp as he walked to the two men. "How can I help you?" he asked Sisto, ignoring Enzo.

"There was a shooting at a business we own."

Enzo stepped close to Mike. "At *Antonio Garage*, outside Vibo."

Mike continued to look at and speak to Sisto as if Enzo was invisible, "Everyone around here is talking about it."

"Do you know who did it?" Sisto asked.

"No, but I have my own opinion of what happened."

Enzo raised his voice. "What?"

When he and Adria had been in the restaurant parking lot, Enzo, the little Mafioso, acted like a big shot.

At the restaurant, he played his part well. Now this little asshole is on my turf. He again spurned Enzo and spoke to Sisto. "The Mafia around here may not like what you are doing and want you to go back to Sicily."

"The Ndrangheta is not the Cosa Nostra!" Enzo shouted.

Mike bit his tongue to keep from laughing but couldn't help smiling at Sisto. "I'm from America. The Ndrangheta, Mafia, and Cosa Nostra are all the same to me. That's all I can tell you."

Sisto nodded. "Enzo will be here in two days. Have the money ready."

This was the opportunity Mike wanted. "I'll have it, but I'm not going to be able to continue paying you." Just as Mike had thought, the men didn't break out in broad smiles.

Enzo stepped beside him and yelled. "Did you hear what he said?"

Mike stared at Sisto, waiting for a reply.

When Enzo kicked Mike's left leg out from under him, he fell to the ground.

Enzo pulled a pistol from under his shirt and planted the muzzle against Mike's forehead. "You may not want to talk to me, American, but you'll pay me when I come, or I'll kill you."

Mike glared at him. "You'll get your money."

Pio ran to Mike's side and helped him stand. He stared at Sisto and Enzo. "There's no need for violence. Mike and I will figure out a way."

Sisto grabbed Enzo's arm. "We're leaving. Don't do anything stupid." The two thugs got into the car and fishtailed down the gravel driveway.

Pio held Mike's arm. "Are you okay?"

"Yeah." He took a deep breath and put a hand on Pio's shoulder. "Jesus! That hurt."

They shuffled into the living room and Mike dropped onto the couch. He pulled up his pant leg and rubbed the welt on the side of his calf.

Gina walked into the room, saw Mike's leg and froze. "My God! Where did you get that welt?"

Pio shook his head. "The little bastard that hit you kicked Mike. He has no brains."

Mike laughed. "I agree. I don't think he could find his way out of a circular room if it had one door." He raised his eyebrows. "I've been thinking about something we need to discuss."

Gina slid beside him and Pio sat in a chair across from them.

"Are people here still as superstitious as our fathers and grandfathers?" Mike glanced at them.

"Everyone in Italy is superstitious," Pio said. "More so in the south."

Gina turned toward Mike. "What does that have to do with our situation?"

"A baker makes bread and turns it upside down after he removes it from the oven. What does that mean?"

She sat up and her eyes widened. "It's the bread of the executioner, no one will touch it... bad luck."

Mike held his fingers together as if holding a coffee cup. "If there are grounds in the bottom of a cup, what would you see?"

"I can't read them and tell the future."

"But some people can," Mike said.

Gina nodded. "Yes. Mostly the older women."

He picked up a pen and note pad from the coffee table and wrote XVII on it. "Okay, now tell me about the number seventeen."

Gina froze, stared at the paper and then at him. "It's bad luck."

He wrote the Roman numeral VIXI on the paper and held it in front of her. "What if I write it like this?"

Gina bit her lip and clamped her hands together on her lap. She stared at the paper.

Pio leaned forward. "Rearranged like that, it says *I have lived* in Latin. It implies *I am now dead*."

"You're scaring me," Gina said.

Mike smiled at Gina. "I didn't think you'd be frightened."

Pio laughed. "Now I know what you're doing."

Gina relaxed. "Oh, I thought you were serious."

"I am. What is the definition of *nemesis*," he asked her.

"An individual or thing that you can't conquer."

Mike nodded. "And *Nemesis* is the Greek Goddess of retribution and revenge."

"What does this have to do with the bastards who killed my father?"

"If I scare them, and one has a heart attack and dies, will I be in trouble?" He looked and Pio and then to Gina.

"No," they said in unison.

"Good idea," Gina said, "but how are we going to frighten them?"

Mike shook his head and smiled. "I'm still trying to figure that out."

That night Mike woke from a sound sleep and bolted upright in bed. He swung his feet to the floor and stared at the wall across the room. *That's it! Beautiful.*

CHAPTER XIV

THE PLAN

Mike leaned against the kitchen counter as Rachele entered.

She smiled. "You're up early."

"I went to bed early." He stepped to the espresso machine. "Sit, I'll make you coffee?"

"Thank you, two sugars, please." She set two large paper bags on the counter and took a seat.

He made two cups, set one in front of her, and sat. "Do we have any loaves of bread?"

She momentarily stared at him and then pointed to the paper bags. "How did you know what I was going to do?"

"What do you mean?"

"I just bought flour and yeast. I plan to make bread this morning."

"See, we think alike." He downed what remained in his cup. "You're making me fat, Rachele, but I love it. I'll see you later."

As he walked out the front door, he spotted Gina standing next to Pio, straddling his motorbike. "No one sleeps late around here." Neither of them were smiling. "What's wrong?"

"Our friend Enzo called." Pio spit on the ground. "He said to have the money ready at four tomorrow afternoon."

Mike nodded and turned to Gina. "Give Rachele the day off tomorrow." He glanced at them. "I have a plan."

"What are we to do?" Gina asked.

Mike placed his hands on her shoulders. The last thing he wanted was to involve his cousin. "Do you trust me?"

"Of course I do! We're family and you're all I have."

"Don't be upset. You need to let Pio and me take care of everything." He stepped back. "If anyone asks, I want you to be able to say you know nothing."

Gina looked at him and paused. "Can I help?"

"You can, by doing as I say. Tomorrow at two, go shopping with one of your friends. You have to be seen in town. Don't come back until after six."

"Are you sure?"

"Yes."

"Okay." She shrugged. "You and Pio talk, I'll go help Rachele."

Mike watched her walk into the house and turned to Pio. "Let's sit on the porch."

He pulled a chair from against the wall and turned it so he and Pio were facing each other. "It's time for Enzo to meet Jesus."

"No." Pio shook his head. "That won't happen. He'll go in the opposite direction. Your uncle was like a brother to me. Let's rid ourselves of this bastard."

Mike stood. "Okay, come."

In Mike's room, he led Pio to the center window. "When Enzo comes, we're taking our money back." He pointed out the window. "See the second intersection on the left? That's where you put the jug of water."

Pio nodded.

"The last time they left here, that's the way they went. I'm hoping Enzo will go the same direction tomorrow. When he stops at the sign, his days stealing from innocent people will come to an end."

Pio didn't do a good job hiding his smile. "You need me to help you here?"

"No. You'll be delivering bread and collecting the payment."

Pio raised his hands and shoulders. "Why the hell am I selling bread?"

Mike laughed. "Relax, you're going to love this."

CHAPTER XV

THE FIRST TARGET

The next morning, Mike walked downstairs and noticed Gina sitting on the couch. She tapped the cushion as he walked to her. "Sit, we'll get coffee in a minute."

"Are you going shopping?" he asked.

"Yes, I'm meeting a friend in Vibo at three. Did you and Pio decide on anything?"

Mike nodded. "I told them I'd pay, so I'm hoping Enzo comes alone."

She stared at him for a moment. "You sure you don't want to tell me about your plan?"

She's smart. She suspects something is about to happen. He shook his head. "It's best. You and I are now the sole owners of the business. If something happens to me, you will own everything. One day you'll marry and have children... Casa Anello is their future. I won't let anyone destroy this family." He watched tears form in her eyes.

She wiped one that slid down her cheek, leaned over, and hugged him. "Thank you."

###

Mike, carrying a loaf of bread, met Pio in the front yard at two-thirty. "Do you have any questions about what you're going to do?"

Pio shook his head. "No. I'll stay at least a hundred meters behind him. Are you sure no one will hear the shot?"

"Positive. It's over a half kilometer from here. Whatever you do, don't hesitate. Come directly back here by the road to the north."

"I will."

Mike held out a loaf and turned it over so Pio could read the letters VIXI burned in the crust. "Set it on the pavement so people see the letters. Is the motorbike ready?"

Pio pointed. "It's behind the office building." He motioned to the bread. "I wouldn't touch that, but I know you were the one who burned VIXI into the bottom." He took the loaf.

"Okay. Be there with your bike at three-thirty and wait, he may come early. Remember the rubber gloves."

Pio placed his hand on Mike's shoulder. "Everything will be fine. You better go upstairs and get ready. Don't forget the money."

Mike walked back into the house and then to his bedroom. He stood at the table in front of the center window and gazed down the hill.

The tripod holding the range finder stood next to the rifle on the table. Both had an unobstructed view of the sign near the stone wall. He leaned to the range finder and rechecked the distance. *Five hundred eleven meters... easy shot.*

Three 250 grain .338 Lapua Magnum rounds stood in a line on the right side of the rifle. *Hopefully I'll only need one.* He inserted the bullets into the magazine and shoved it into the well below the bolt.

He removed 5,500 Euros wrapped in a rubber band from the center drawer of the desk and went downstairs.

In the living room he saw Pio writing something on an empty envelope. "Everything okay?"

"Yes. Here, this is for the money."

Mike took it and looked at what Pio had written. He had not noticed Casa Anello, and the date written on the envelope the last time he had paid Sisto. "Why did you write this?"

"Everyone has been told to do the same so these assholes can tell who paid and who didn't."

Mike stuffed the euros into the envelope and sealed it. He looked at his watch. "Three-thirty, you better go. I'll wait on the porch."

He sat in a chair near the front door and stared at the charred debris of the shed that once stood in front of Gina's vacant parking space. When he made the decision to ship his rifle to Italy, his intention had been to continue to hone his shooting skills. Long distance shooting was an art. Until he thought about the Alexander Pope's quote, *Behold on wrong swift vengeance waits,* he hadn't realized what he had to do. Killing his uncle, an innocent man, had been the *wrong,* the MRAD .338 Lapua was the *swift vengeance.*

The whine of an approaching motorcycle interrupted his thoughts. He remained seated as Enzo came up the driveway and stopped in front of the house. The leather shoulder bag hung at his side.

Mike limped from the porch, stopped in front of the Ducati, and stared at the little Mafioso.

Enzo removed his black helmet and held out his hand. "The money."

Mike pulled the envelope from his back pocket and held it out, but didn't move.

The thug lowered the kickstand, walked to him, and took it. "Next time you hand it to me so I don't have to get off of my motorcycle."

Mike nodded. "I promise you, it will never happen again."

"Did you add five hundred?"

"I did what you asked."

Enzo smiled. "Where is the pretty girl who lives here? I want to see her."

"That's not possible."

"Why not?"

"She's in church praying for the souls of the dead." Expressionless, he looked into Enzo's eyes. "Good day." He walked to the front door, entered and slammed it shut.

As the sound of the motorcycle receded, he hurried upstairs to his bedroom, hit the play button on the stereo, and opened the window.

Rod Stewart's *Rhythm of my Heart* began to play as Mike positioned himself behind the rifle and chambered a round. He leaned to the range finder. Enzo reached the end of the driveway and stopped for a passing truck. As planned, Pio followed at a safe distance.

Enzo turned onto the paved road and headed toward the first intersection. Mike leaned over the rifle, adjusted his right eye behind the scope and followed the motorcycle.

Enzo came to a full stop and looked in both directions. *Not your typical Italian driver.* Mike placed his finger on the trigger, slowed his breathing and followed the bike to the second sign. The moment Enzo stopped at the intersection, Mike took aim. He placed the crosshairs on the back of the helmet, squeezed the trigger and heard the crack of a single shot.

Enzo's head slammed forward, and he toppled to the pavement as the bike fell.

Within seconds, Pio stopped beside the fallen Ducati and snatched the leather pouch from the dead man. He removed the loaf of bread from a bag hanging on his handlebars and set it upside down beside the body. Pio then made a quick right turn onto the intersecting road and sped away.

Mike focused on the growing pool of blood under Enzo's twisted body. *You picked on the wrong family.* He ejected the spent cartridge and removed the magazine from the rifle. After placing the weapon in the hidden storage space, he moved the dresser back into place and walked to the window.

Without his range finder or a pair of binoculars he could not clearly see Enzo's lifeless body a half kilometer from the villa. He stared at the distant intersection. *Pope spoke of vengeance, but avenge may be a more appropriate word. The intent is to punish evil behavior and see justice done.* He closed the window and headed downstairs to wait for Pio.

CHAPTER XVI

THE MONEY

Mike waited on the porch. It didn't take Pio long to get back to the house.

He parked the motorbike in front of a van. With a grin, he removed the rubber gloves and strolled toward the house holding Enzo's bag. "I was worried the police may find the bullet, but it went right through him." He handed Mike the bag.

"Two thousand five hundred feet per second, Pio. Enzo's empty head wasn't going to stop it." He turned to the door. "Let's go in and see what treasures this bag holds."

Mike sat on the couch, and Pio across from him. He opened the satchel and removed nine envelopes. When he found the one marked Casa Anello, he shoved it in his pocket. "We paid him, but the poor bastard was robbed by an unscrupulous criminal."

Pio pointed at the remaining envelopes. "What are we going to do with those?"

Mike shrugged and grinned. "Maybe a Calabrian Robin Hood will return them to the people."

"There are many myths around here, but I don't think a Robin Hood figure is one of them."

"Then we must create one." He handed the envelopes to Pio. "Keep these in a safe place. We need to figure out a way to return the money without people connecting it to us." He threw the bag to him. "Destroy this so it won't be found."

After Pio left, Mike sat in the living room and followed a game show on television. Two young women in sexy outfits used one hand to scoop water out of a bucket and fill as many plastic cups as possible in one minute. A middle-aged male host seemed to be enjoying the outfit drenching spectacle. *Won't find anything like this on CBS.*

Gina hurried through the front door just as the program ended. "The police are down the road!"

"What happened?"

"There's a crowd. The man that lives in the nearby house told me someone was shot."

Mike stood and raised his eyebrows. "Maybe the local clans got tired of Mafia members on motorcycles."

Gina stared at him for a full five seconds. "You knew it was a man on a Ducati motorcycle?"

"Let's just say it was a wild guess."

"Did he come here and did you pay him?"

"Yes. He carried a shoulder bag. If the police got the money, they'll be asking questions. Best if we keep quiet. We don't want the Mafia to get suspicious."

Gina paused while looking at him. "There's one more thing. The man told me a loaf of bread lay upside down next to the body." She raised her eyebrows. "He said VIXI had been burned into the crust."

Mike shrugged and raised his open palms. "What a coincidence, we talked about that the other day. The executioner's bread and the Latin term 'I have lived'. I'll bet the dead guy's superstitious friends are going to worry."

Gina held up her index finger. "Mike, I know what—"

"Gina." Mike looked at her and pressed his lips together. "Don't."

She nodded. "I understand, but I have one question. Will this work?"

"We'll go on with our lives and wait to see."

Three days after his nephew died, Bortolo sat at a back table in *Lo Spirito* and thumbed through cards and notes of condolence scattered in front of him. Unable to concentrate on the words, he lifted a bottle of Jameson Caskmates Irish Whiskey and filled his glass.

Enzo's funeral was scheduled in two days, and he dreaded facing his sister for the second time in a week. His decision to honor her request, and take Enzo under his wing, haunted him. The kid's friends had teased him about how short he was and referred to him as *Mezza Bottiglia* behind his back. *Half a bottle... those had been fighting words to him.*

Bortolo had no idea it would come to this. He pounded his fist on the table. He'd tried to convince his sister that her son should seek a trade. The kid's little-man complex had resulted in cuts and bruises, and Bortolo knew one day he'd open his mouth to the wrong person. The two things that made his blood boil were how his nephew had been killed, and the word *vixi* scored on the upside down loaf of bread next to his body. *Who's the peasant who thinks he's the executioner?*

As Sisto approached his table, Bortolo noticed beads of sweat on his forehead. He pointed to a chair, and downed half the liquor in his glass. "Sit and relax, you're not in trouble."

Sisto dropped into the chair. "I'm sorry we must meet under sad circumstances."

"No one should have to bury his children or young family members. Have you found out anything?"

"No. The local police called in the Carabinieri. Once they identified him and found out he lived in Messina, they began to look into why he was in Vibo." He paused and took a deep breath. "It didn't take long to discover he was related to you. They're trying to figure out what he was doing in Calabria. They are talking to people who live near where he was shot."

Bortolo twisted the black onyx ring on his pinky finger. "Do they know of our arrangements with the local clans?"

"I don't think so."

"Is it possible the Ndrangheta killed him?"

Sisto paused and furrowed his brow. "I doubt it, but it could have been anyone. The people talk to each other. It's common knowledge that he carried large sums of cash."

Bortolo bit his lip and stared at the table top. *The clans did it, or the damn locals took their money back.* "I want answers, Sisto. Take two of my men with you. Meet with the clan leader in Vibo and tell him I will avenge my nephew's murder. Observe him closely when you speak to him. Tell me what he says... how he acts."

"I'll make arrangements to see him tomorrow."

"Do we have friends with the local police?"

"Yes, but now that the Carabinieri are involved, it won't be easy to find out what is going on with the investigation."

"The American you and Enzo mentioned? Could he have had something to do with it?"

"No." Sisto shook his head. "Whoever planned Enzo's murder, knew what they were doing and did it quickly. The guy limps. He couldn't move fast enough. Not with that leg."

"Could it have been someone else in his family?"

"There's only his cousin. Her name is Gina. The business manager's name is Pio. He often appears angry, and may be capable of murder."

Bortolo wanted pressure put on the Calabrian's, but he recalled what had happened in 2007 and 2008. The head of the Mafia family in Palermo, Salvatore Lo Piccolo, was arrested. A list of businesses that paid him protection money was found in his desk. The citizens became outraged, banded together and stood up to the Mafia by refusing to pay. *Calabrians don't have the balls, but I must be cautious.* "I want you to send a message to the business owners in Vibo.

If they don't do what we say, there will be hell to pay." He thrust a finger at Sisto. "Let the people know we want our money. Make them pay for what happened and do it now. Talk with this man named Pio. Find out if he has any information about the shooting. If he does, I want him brought here. If he knows nothing, at least he'll find out how serious we are, and he'll tell the others."

CHAPTER XVII

SISTO STRIKES

It didn't take Sisto long to track down Pio in Vibo Valentia.

Two nights later he sat in a car outside R&P Metal Fabrication. Dante and Leone, two men from Bortolo's organization, were with him.

Sisto glanced at his watch. "It's almost nine, he won't stay much longer. Remember, I don't want him killed. If he knows anything about Enzo's murder, we'll take him to Messina."

"If he does, we should bury him in the hills." Leone said.

Sisto looked into the rearview mirror and glared at the bearded man in the back seat. "Great." He shook his head. "When we see the boss again, we'll tell him it was your idea."

Leone squirmed and shook his head. "No, forget what I said."

"Let's go." Sisto opened his door. "We'll wait for him."

They hid behind a truck parked next to the Anello company van.

When Sisto saw their target come out the door, he whispered. "That's him." He stepped from behind the truck. "Good evening."

Pio stopped and glared when he recognized Sisto and noticed the two men standing beside him. "What do you want?"

Sisto smiled. "To talk."

"You have your money. What do you want from me?" He planted his feet shoulder width apart and stood his ground.

Sisto and Leone stepped in front of him and Dante moved to his side. "Our friend's murder," Sisto said. "You seem to be able to take care of yourself. I think you may know who killed Enzo and stole from me. It happened less than a kilometer from where you work."

Pio raised both hands and shrugged. "Many things happen in Vibo. It doesn't mean I did them. I was working and didn't find out what happened until nine that night."

Leone planted his index finger against Pio's chest. "Don't lie to us, Calabrese!"

Pio threw a right hook that landed on Leone's jaw with a thud.

The Mafioso's knees gave out, and he crumpled to the ground.

Dante didn't hesitate. He pulled a wooden club from his waistband and slammed it against Pio's thigh. As he dropped to his knees, Dante's leather boot struck the side of his head.

Mike woke early the next morning and looked at his watch. *Damn, 4:00 AM.* He pulled on a pair of cargo pants, sat at the desk, and thought of recent events. He realized Gina suspected he and Pio had something to do with Enzo's death and knew she wouldn't breathe a word to anyone. In spite of the gossip about the shooting, life in and around Vibo had returned to normal.

Quick footsteps in the hall outside his room made him turn towards the door.

Gina burst into the room screaming. "Mike! One of our vans is on fire!" She turned and ran.

He grabbed a T-shirt and thundered down the stairs.

Gina, her hand covering her mouth, stood at the open front door.

He glanced at the glow in the sky, and the van, half engulfed in flames. "A hose!" He grabbed her arm. "Is there a hose?"

"Yes!" She ran to the side of the house and he followed.

Mike pulled the hose from a short wooden barrel and turned on the faucet. He raced toward the van. Ten feet from the fire, the nozzle flew from his hand. *Dammit! Not long enough.* He picked up the hose and opened the nozzle until a stream of water reached the flames.

Gina stopped beside him. "Should I get a bucket?"

"No!" He pointed at her car in the parking space next to the van. "Get the keys to your Mercedes." He turned back to the burning vehicle and visualized the explosion when the flames reached the gas tank.

Gina returned and started past him. "I'll move the car!"

Mike stuck out his arm and stopped her. He handed her the hose and grabbed the keys out of her hand. "Spray near the back bumper. After I move the car, drop the hose and run, that thing might explode."

He raced to the side of the van and removed the gas cap. He then jumped into the Mercedes, shoved the car into reverse, and hit the gas. As the car skidded to a stop a safe distance from the burning van, he threw open the door and leapt out. "Gina! Run to the house."

Mike stopped beside his cousin. "Is the gas tank full?"

"I don't know. We fill them once a week."

"It shouldn't explode now. Did you call the fire department?"

"They said there were too many fires tonight and it may take more than an hour to get here."

Mike looked at the fully engulfed van and shook his head. "The tank must be almost empty. There's nothing more we can do. Let's go inside."

By nine, Mike and Gina sat in the living room.

"When will Pio be here?" he asked.

"He said he'd be late, maybe noon."

They looked at each other when they heard the roar of an approaching motor.

Gina looked out the window. "It's a fire truck and the Carabinieri."

As they walked outside, Mike exaggerated his limp.

Two young Carabinieri approached while several firemen casually deployed a hose and sprayed a weak stream of water on what remained of the smoldering van.

The two officers in uniform wore black red striped pants and light blue shirts.

The tall one, with well-trimmed stubble on his chin, spoke. "Good morning, I'm Mario Daleo." He pointed at his partner who looked to be ten years his junior. "This is Benito Flori. May we have a word with you?"

"I'm Mike Anello, and this is my cousin, Gina Anello." He shook hands with the two officers. "The Carabinieri are concerned with someone setting fire to a van?"

"That and other things," Daleo said. "Do both of you live here?"

Mike nodded. "Yes. I recently arrived. I also live in the United States, but I'm an Italian citizen. Gina and I are the owners of Casa Anello Olive Oil."

"How long will you be staying in Calabria?" Flori asked.

Mike lifted his hands, palms raised. "This is my home. I may not return to America."

"Many fires were set last night." Daleo took a deep breath. "Thank God no one was killed."

"Do you have any idea who did this?" Flori asked. "Is someone angry at you," he pointed at the van, "or your business?"

Both said "No."

Daleo rubbed the growth on his chin. "I noticed you were limping. Would you be more comfortable sitting?"

"I'm fine, but let's go in the house."

When they walked into the living room and sat, Mike glanced a Gina. *She's not afraid of them... quite calm.*

"Would you like coffee?" Gina asked.

Daleo shook his head. "No. A man was recently shot near here. Do either of you know him, he's from Messina?"

"That day I returned from shopping with a friend. On my way home I saw the crowd near the intersection," Gina said. "I stopped and spoke with a man who lives nearby."

Mike tapped his left leg. "It wasn't a good day for me. I was in a lot of pain and took medication. Spent most of the time in my bedroom or here in the living room. Did you find out who killed him?"

"No, but it's odd," Daleo said. "His family in Messina is wealthy, and he may have been a member of the Mafia."

"Mafia?" Mike furrowed his brow. "Why would he be in Calabria?"

Flori shrugged. "We don't know yet."

Gina locked her eyes on him. "It's always been safe around here. We don't want anything happening to us or our employees. What are you going to do?"

Daleo leaned toward her. "Two officers from the Special Operations Group in Reggio are coming here to help. They are familiar with the activities of the Ndrangheta and the Costa Nostra. Do either of you own any weapons?"

Mike shook his head and glanced at Gina.

"Yes. My father recently died, and his shotgun is in the house. He used it to hunt."

"We heard of his death." Daleo nodded. "Sorry for your loss. The gun is registered?"

"Yes, in Vibo."

Flori stared at her. "Is that the only gun?"

"Yes."

Mike did not react to Gina's lie. *Yeah, except for the two German submachine guns and my long shooter. She's good.*

Daleo nodded. "Last night, five vehicles and sheds were set on fire at businesses and farms in the area. Do you have any idea why someone would do this?"

Gina shook her head.

"No," Mike said. "Do you?"

Both Carabinieri hesitated, and Daleo leaned forward in his chair. "People are talking about paying the Mafia for protection. You want to tell us what you know?"

Mike stared at the senior officer. *He's trying to act intimidating. Two can play that game.* He sat up and, leaned to the officer. "My uncle," he pointed at his cousin, "Gina's father, was recently murdered. Has his killer been found?"

Both officer's shook their heads.

Mike did not take his eyes off of Daleo. "Are you married?"

"Yes."

"Do you have children?"

"I don't think that matters."

Mike raised an index finger. "It does! If your family lived in this house, miles from the nearest police officer, would they be safe talking about what is happening around here?"

Daleo pressed his lips together. Neither officer said a word.

"You know what is going on. When you find my uncles killer, and you get the Mafia out of our pockets, come back and we'll talk."

Both officers stood and Daleo looked at Mike. "Thank you for speaking with us. Give us time, we'll solve the murders, and find out who set the fires." They walked to the door.

When his cell phone rang, Daleo stopped and answered it. After a short low conversation he turned to Gina and Mike. "Pio Baldi works for you?"

"Yes," Gina replied.

"He was found unconscious in a parking lot and treated at the hospital. He's home now."

Gina jumped up. "What happened?"

"Someone attacked him outside a metal shop. He was badly beaten."

As soon as the Carabinieri left, Gina pulled out her cell phone. "We need to go see if he's okay and find out what happened. I'll call Camilla."

CHAPTER XVIII

DECISION TIME

Gina and Mike arrived at Pio's house an hour later.

Camilla answered the door. "He doesn't need to stay in bed but he's tired... the pain keeps him from sleeping." She led them to the master bedroom.

Pio, with a pillow behind him, leaned against the headboard.

Gina rushed to his side and kissed his cheek. "Are you okay?"

Pio grinned and then moaned and touched his jaw. "Yes. A little sore and a broken rib."

Mike walked to the foot of the bed. "Did someone try to rob you?"

"No. Sisto and two of his friends waited for me outside the metal shop. They wanted to know if I knew anything about Enzo being killed."

Mike shook his head. "Looks as if they didn't like your answer." Mike could tell Pio was trying not to smile, but his eyes gave away his sense of pleasure.

"They didn't, but I threw the first punch. I may have broken the guy's jaw. I don't remember him getting up."

Mike glanced at Camilla and Gina. "Do you mind if I speak to Pio alone?"

The women nodded and left the room.

Pio described everything that happened and what was said. He told Mike the last thing he remembered was being kicked as he lay on the ground. "I found out Sisto works for the Mafia boss in Messina. His name is Bortolo Umbro."

Mike nodded and bit his lower lip. "What do you know about him?"

"Nothing, but there's a bartender in Vibo who can tell you quite a bit. His name is Imo, he's married to my wife's cousin."

"Can he be trusted?"

"Yes. His son is my godchild. Sisto and the other Sicilians go into the bar often."

Mike pulled a chair beside the bed and sat. "What's the name of this place?"

"Stromboli... like the volcano off the coast of Italy. Don't go there. I'll make arrangements for him to meet you someplace else."

Mike concluded that he needed to be proactive and send a message to the Mafia boss and his crew. "These bastards are concerned they'll lose the money they are extorting. I want to make them think the Ndrangheta clans are behind Enzo's death. Maybe they'll start killing each other."

"I'll feel better tomorrow. We'll both meet Imo."

"No. Take your time and regain your strength. Call me after you talk with him." Mike walked to the door and called Gina and Camilla. They talked for the next half hour, but avoided the subject of the Mafia.

Gina remained quiet on the way home. She stared out the windshield and tapped her fingers against her leg.

Mike pulled onto the dirt road leading to the villa.

She turned to him. "Should we sell Casa Anello?"

Mike slowed the car and looked at her. "That's not going to happen. No one will destroy what our parents and grandparents, worked so hard to build. Our grandmother spent years picking olives in these groves. As long as they are getting what they want from us, there won't be a problem."

"How can we afford to continue paying five thousand euros a month? They won't stop until they've taken everything and we're dead!" She covered her mouth as soon as the words came out. "I'm sorry. They scare me."

Mike parked in front of the house. *More scared than I thought.* "If I tell you we can afford it, will you believe me and stop worrying?"

She shrugged. "Yes."

"Good. We can afford it." He paused and smiled. "I'll make plans to disrupt their extortion scheme."

When they reached the porch, he grabbed the door handle and stopped. "I need to get something from my room and then I'm going to the metal shop in Vibo."

Gina's eyes widened. "Your rifle?"

Mike smiled. "No, that thing is too big." He held the door for her, and then headed upstairs.

CHAPTER XIX

DANCE BORTOLO

The next morning, Mike met Imo in an isolated olive grove a few miles from the villa.

After a few minutes of casual conversation, Mike got to the point. "Tell me about the Sicilians that come into your bar."

Imo raised his eyebrows and looked around. "If Sisto finds out we spoke, I'll be dead."

Mike rested his hand on the young man's shoulder. "You have nothing to worry about. Your child's godfather has been with Casa Anello for a long time. His father and my uncle were like brothers."

Imo nodded. "Romeo's death hurt Pio. My wife and I attended his funeral."

"It should have never happened. If he had told me the Mafia was extorting him, I would have been here the next day."

"You probably know Sisto is the leader of the group in Vibo," Imo said. "Normally there are three or four of them, but in the last week two more men came. I think they are the ones who beat Pio."

"Do you know their names?"

Imo shook his head. "Not all of them, but two stay close to Sisto. He called them Dante and Leone. Leone has a beard, and he's much shorter than Dante."

"What about their boss in Messina? Pio told me his name is Bortolo Umbro."

"Yes, Sisto told me of him. He's only been to my bar once... the day after Enzo was killed. He came in a new black Mercedes." Imo took a deep breath. "Whoever killed Enzo better be careful. Bortolo said the person who identifies the killer will get a three thousand euros."

Mike shrugged. "He carried a lot of money. I'll bet one of the clans had something to do with it. What does Bortolo look like?"

"He's easy to recognize. The same height as you, but much heavier... a fat ass. His head is shaved, and he has a black mustache and a goatee."

"How old is he?"

"Fifty-five or sixty." He shrugged.

Mike glanced to the ground and paused. "If someone wanted to talk to him, where would they find him in Messina?"

"That person would be crazy. He owns a bar, *Lo Spirito*. I've been told he's there every night during the week and leaves between ten-thirty and eleven."

Mike stared at him for a moment. "How do you know this?"

"Sisto loves to talk, and I listen. He hopes one day to be Bortolo's right-hand man."

"Where's the bar located?"

"Sisto said it's in a section they call the New Quarters... west of the train terminal." Imo raised his hands and shook his head. "I don't know the street."

"Which one? The Messina Centrale station?"

"Yes."

They talked for a few minutes about Imo's family, but Mike couldn't wait to get home.

When he reached the villa, he raced to his room, turned on the computer and googled Bortolo Umbro.

It took him an hour to find Italian newspaper articles about the Mafia in and around Messina. After he printed two photos of Bortolo, he left Gina a note. He told her he had taken a company van and wouldn't return until after midnight. By three-thirty he had dressed head-to-toe in black, packed what he needed, and drove off in the van.

He caught the seven-twenty ferry from Reggio to Messina, and by ten he stood in the shadows of an alley across from *Lo Spirito*. A black Mercedes was parked in front of the bar. *If Imo's correct, that's his car.*

Mike had to stifle a laugh when his saw Bortolo walk out. *Fat! Imo hit the nail on the head. He's as round as he is tall.* He slipped a nine millimeter pistol with a silencer from his waistband, waited for Bortolo to get into the car and start the engine.

Mike took aim and fired a single shot into the pavement near the front tire. Bullet fragments tore into the tire and the left front of the car dropped onto the rim.

Bortolo flung open the door and didn't bother to turn off the engine when he struggled out. He bent over, examined the flat, and yelled cuss words, loud enough for Mike to hear each vile term. As Bortolo stood, Mike fired a second shot into the pavement behind his feet, knowing the bullets ricochet would hobble the fat man.

The round struck the street kicking shrapnel and stone into Bortolo's feet and ankles. The Mafioso screamed in agony as he fell to the pavement.

Mike picked up the two spent cartridge casings and disappeared into the dark alley.

###

The day after the shooting, Bortolo, with both feet wrapped in bandages, sat in a wheelchair at the back of *Lo Spirito*. He motioned to a chair as a local police officer approached.

"Thank you for coming, Massimo." He slid an envelope across the table. "What have the police found out in the past twenty-four hours?"

Massimo took a seat, picked up the envelope, and shoved it into his pocket. "Nothing that will help us find the asshole. You're lucky he didn't hit you. He had to be an amateur. Are you sure you didn't hear a gunshot?"

Bortolo leaned forward and locked eyes with Massimo. "I'm not deaf, I heard nothing."

"We found bullet fragments and believe it was a nine millimeter. No casings were found."

"Maybe it was a revolver."

"I doubt it. We don't see many nine millimeter revolvers. They're rare."

"Are your men talking to everyone in the neighborhood?"

"Yes, but no one saw anything out of the ordinary."

"I'm paying you a lot to keep me informed. I want a call the minute you find out who did this." He shoved his wheelchair away from the table indicating their conversation had ended.

Massimo stood. "We'll find the guy." He walked out of the bar.

Bortolo motioned to one of his men. "Where's Sisto?"

"In the back room."

"Get him and bring me a bottle of whiskey and two glasses."

Sisto dropped into the chair across from him. "Thank God the man wasn't a good shot. I hope you're feeling better."

Bortolo filled two small glasses and slid one across the table. "This and the medication helps, but I'm still mad. The shooter has a better aim than we give him credit for."

Sisto downed his drink. "The bullet missed. If he had been any good, he would have killed you."

"No, Sisto. Think about something." He refilled both glasses. "What are the chances the same thing happened to me that happened to the men at the garage in Vibo?"

Sisto's eyes widened. "You're right!"

Bortolo pulled a paper from his pocket. "Who found this?" He waved the two pages and slid them across the table.

"The man who repaired your tire. It was taped to the front license plate."

"Do you know what it means?"

Sisto stared at a picture of a loaf of bread laying upside down on a wooden table. "Yes, it's the executioner's bread."

"And the word burned into the crust?"

Sisto's took a deep breath. "It's Latin, 'I have lived', which implies I am now dead. It's the same as the one found near Enzo's body."

"Turn the page," Bortolo said.

Sisto read the words typed on the paper. "Behold, on wrong swift vengeance waits." He dropped the papers and pulled his hands away from the table. His mouth fell open, and he stared at what he had read. "What are you going to do?"

Bortolo picked up the pages and returned them to his pocket. "He thinks he is going to scare me, but we know more than the police. Someone near Vibo Valentia has a steady hand and more balls than they do brains. Have your men start asking questions... do whatever is necessary. I want this bastard found before he decides to raise his aim."

"The guy we sent to the hospital couldn't tell us anything, and his boss, the American, can't help us. He's useless."

Bortolo scrunched his eyebrows and tilted his head. "Useless?"

"Yes. His leg, remember I told you he's crippled."

Bortolo nodded. "Put pressure on the people who pay us. Someone had to see something. Since our money was stolen, tell them we'll collect again to make up for what was taken. If anyone dares to refuse, call me. I'll change their minds."

Two days later, Mike sat in the living room with cell phone earbuds in his ears. Out of the corner of his eyes he saw Pio walk into the house. He tapped the screen of the phone, removed the buds, and stood. "What are you doing out of bed?" He motioned to a large armchair. "Sit here."

Pio moaned as he eased into the chair. "I'm bored and we need to talk about what happened."

"How do you feel?"

"A lot better than twenty-four hours ago."

Mike tightened his jaw and stared at Pio's black eye and bruised face. "Rachele is shopping. You want coffee, or something stronger?"

"Whiskey, but not Grappa."

Mike walked to a cabinet, opened a door and grabbed a bottle of Vecchia Romagna Brandy and two glasses. He handed Pio a glass, poured a generous amount, and sat across from him.

"They are not going to quit, Mike. Their boss in Messina won't stop until he finds out who killed his nephew."

Mike grinned. At that moment he realized Pio had not watched television while recuperating. "You missed the news out of Messina. They're reporting someone tried to kill Bortolo Umbro."

Pio sat up. "What happened?"

"It seems the assassin didn't do a good job. The bullet hit the street and fragments tore into chubby ankles and feet.

Pio grabbed his side and moaned as he laughed. "Gina told me you disappeared one night until three in the morning. She said you wouldn't explain where you had been. Tell me what happened."

"I went to visit him at his bar. It's called *Lo Spirito*."

Pio's eyes widened. "You spoke with him?"

"No. Remember the two guards I made dance at the garage?"

"Yes." Pio grinned. "I wish I had seen it."

"I arranged for him to prance to the same music."

Pio's mouth dropped open. "You took your rifle to Sicily?"

"No. I made a silencer for one of the pistols. The hour wait outside his bar was worth it. I put one round into the cobblestones a few feet behind where he was standing. It tore up his ankles, and when I left he was squealing like a pig and pulling off both his shoes."

Pio sighed. "Did he see you?"

"Hell no! But I did leave him a photo to make him worry."

"Of what?"

"An upside down loaf of bread with VIXI burned into the crust."

When Pio laughed and doubled over in pain, Mike thought it best if he quit with the humor.

Pio leaned back in the chair and smiled. "I bet he shit his pants."

Mike pressed his lips together. "I decided what I'm going to do. We need to stick together and we should be able to make them leave us and everyone else alone. Once a few more of them die, they'll decide it's not worth it."

"What do you have planned?"

"When are they coming for the next payment?"

Pio raised his shoulders. "I'm not sure. It hasn't been that long since Enzo departed for hell."

"Hopefully they won't make people replace what was taken from them. We'll be patient and wait. Do they always leave the villa and drive in the same direction?"

"Yes, the same road Enzo used, but if they are going to the others, they may turn right and go east on the paved road."

Mike tightened his jaw and nodded. "It doesn't matter which way they turn. They'll have to stop at an intersection. I prefer they come here last. Let's make sure that happens."

CHAPTER XX

THE NEXT PAYMENT

Pio took another couple of days off to recover and finally felt he could return to work. On his way to the villa he turned off the road and started up the long driveway.

The ring of his cell phone startled him. He looked at the screen. *What does this asshole want? I hope they didn't find out about Imo.* On the third ring he answered the call. "Hello."

"It's Sisto. I hope you're well."

Pio pressed his lips together. "I am. What do you want?"

"We're coming to collect on Thursday. Have five thousand ready for Dante and Leone."

"Who the hell are they?"

Sisto chuckled. "You met them in the parking lot outside the metal shop."

Pio paused and shook his head. *He thinks I'm frightened.* "We paid you this month! Where are we supposed to get 5,000 euros?"

"I don't give a shit, Pio. One of your friends stole from us. Get it from him."

Pio's eyes widened. *Remember what Mike said.* "We'll be out of town and won't be back until late afternoon."

Sisto didn't respond.

"You still there?"

"Yes. I'll tell them to come after four." He ended the call.

When Pio walked into the house, he found Mike at a laptop on the dining room table. "Sisto, called. He wants another payment Thursday to make up for what they didn't get. He's sending the two guys that I fought with outside the R&P metal shop. Their names are Dante and Leone."

Mike took a breath. "Greedy bastards, aren't they?"

Pio nodded. "I told him we wouldn't be here until four."

Mike smiled. "Good. We'll do it the same way we did last time. They should have already collected envelopes from the others. Where did you put the cash we got from Enzo?"

"It's at my house."

"Once these bastards decide to leave Calabria, we'll need to figure out how we can return the cash to everyone. I'll talk to Gina and send her to Vibo for another day of shopping."

Mike and Pio spent the next morning planning. Since two people were coming to get the money, they figured the men would be in a car.

This time Pio was not going to follow them. He'd hide himself, and his motorbike, in the trees and brush along the stone wall at the second stop sign.

Before noon, Mike and Pio hid long 4x4 pieces of wood and concrete blocks at the base of the wall.

Thursday morning Mike and Pio again discussed what they'd do.

By three-thirty, Pio had left the villa and went to his hiding place. Mike, wearing cargo shorts and a golf shirt sat in a chair on the porch. He glanced at his watch when he saw the Fiat approach the house.

When the car stopped, both men got out.

Pio said Leone had the beard. Dante's the driver. Mike limped from the porch and stopped in front of the two men. He decided to be uncooperative and did not smile. "Hello. What can I do for you?"

Leone looked at his clean-shaven partner and turned to Mike. "Sisto sent us."

"Oh. Then you must be Dante and Leone. Pio told me to expect you."

Dante nodded. "You have something for us?"

"I do, but I want you to deliver a message to Sisto. I don't have much money left to pay for protection."

Leone stepped in front of him. "Your friend Pio was lucky. If the same thing happens to you, the hospital will be the last place you visit."

"You're getting it today. Tell Sisto I want to talk to him." He handed Leone the envelope and watched him stuff it into a red cloth shopping bag.

Both thugs walked to the car. Before Dante opened his door, he looked at Mike. "Sisto is busy. He doesn't have time for you."

Mike shrugged and raised his hands. "Give him the message and let him decide if he wants to talk." He turned, limped into the house, and tapped the screen of his cell phone. Pio answered on the second ring.

"Yes, Mike."

"Leone put the money in a red shopping bag. They're leaving now."

"I'll block the road. I hope no one else comes before they get there." Pio said.

Mike hurried into his bedroom and glanced at the rifle and binoculars on the table in front of the open window. He stepped to the stereo, hit the play button, and sat in the chair behind the weapon. He lifted the stock of his rifle, pressed the butt against his shoulder and adjusted his eye behind the scope. Sade's *Smooth Operator* began to play, but he paid little attention to the words.

The Fiat came into view in the scope. It accelerated from the first stop sign and headed toward the blocked intersection. The car stopped ten feet in front of the wood and cement blocks that covered the road.

Mike focused on the rear window and saw the two men talking inside the car. *What the hell are they doing... hope they don't turn around.*

Dante pointed and Leone opened his door and headed to the debris.

Mike centered the crosshairs on the back of his head.

Leone stopped next to a wooden 4x4, turned and looked at Dante.

The words of Sade's song suddenly overcame the music. Mike squeezed the trigger.

Leone's head snapped back as his body dropped to the pavement.

He chambered a second round, repositioned his scope and focused on Dante, who was scrambling to get out of the car. He knew the man could not have heard the shot, and would wonder what happened to his friend.

The Mafioso ran to Leone and knelt beside him.

The second shot hit Dante just below his ear. He lurched forward, falling on top of his dead partner.

Mike stood and grabbed the binoculars.

Pio stopped his motorbike beside the car. He leaned the bike against the rear door and snatched the red bag from inside the Fiat. A second later he turned the bike around and sped toward the villa.

Mike dashed down the stairs and stopped on the porch.

Pio pulled in front of the house and approached with a grim expression on his face.

"Are you okay?" Mike asked.

"Yes. It wasn't pretty... nothing I want to see again."

"Remember what Romeo looked like when you found his body?"

Pio looked at the ground. "They beat him so bad I didn't recognize him."

Mike placed a hand on Pio's shoulder. "He suffered, Pio, the two down the road felt nothing. Imagine how long it took my uncle to die." He motioned toward the front door. "Hide the bag in the house and let's go have a drink. I'll meet you in the van."

Pio nodded and stepped through the door.

Mike climbed into the passenger seat and waited. *The shit is going to hit the fan when Bortolo finds out.*

Pio got behind the wheel and drove the ten miles to Pizzo where he found a parking place near Piazza della Republica. The two men had remained silent during the trip. They walked to a side street and entered *The Stone Bell.* Pio led Mike past the rustic bar to a table along the back wall.

Mike looked around the bar. "Nice place."

Pio smiled. "It's one of the best pubs in Pizzo. The pizza is good and they serve local craft beers."

A young woman pulled out a chair at the table next to them.

A man at the adjacent table jumped up and shoved her. "Sit somewhere else! I want that left vacant for my friends."

Mike stood and stepped behind the man.

Pio moved to Mike's side as he spun the guy around and jammed a finger into the man's chest.

"Why don't you try to push me?" Mike pointed at the man's empty chair. "Sit and enjoy yourself. She's a friend of mine, and if you touch her again, I'll break your arm."

The guy plunked down and grumbled while looking away.

Mike motioned to the empty chairs where he and Pio had been sitting. "Sit there. My friend and I will take the table next to you." He held a chair for her.

"Thank you," she said.

A couple of minutes after he and Pio took the vacant seats, the man who had pushed the woman got up, mumbled to himself, and walked across the room.

Pio leaned forward and lowered his voice. "Be careful. Everyone is looking at us. You'll get in trouble. I've never seen that guy around here... he may have friends in Sicily."

"I'm getting to the point where I don't care... but I agree with you. We shouldn't draw attention to ourselves."

Pio lowered his voice to a whisper. "For the second time, Sisto and his men got nothing. The boss in Messina isn't going to sit on his ass."

CHAPTER XXI

THE LIE

Three days after his men were killed, Bortolo and Sisto sat at a table in *Lo Spirito* and drank coffee.

A cane leaned against the side of the boss' chair. He raised his hand and held up his index finger. "I received a call about the crippled American in Vibo. He had a confrontation with a tourist in a local bar called *The Stone Bell*. For a man with a bad leg, he acted as if he could take care of himself."

Sisto furrowed his brow. "How do you know?"

"One of the waiters keeps his eyes open for me. This guy has bigger balls than we thought. Not many people know, but I've been told his was injured while in Afghanistan."

"Then he lied to me." Sisto slapped the table. "He said it happened in a motorcycle accident."

"Have another conversation with him. This time keep your eyes and ears open."

Mike down-shifted the Jeep as he came to a turn in the road leading to the villa. In the rearview mirror he noticed a black van approaching. He turned his eyes back to the curve in front of him.

Halfway into it, the van pulled beside him, forcing his Jeep to the side of the road. It then stopped in front of him, blocking his path.

He threw open his door and got out. *Where'd this guy get his license?*

Sisto and another man got out of the van.

Mike purposely limped toward him. "Are you crazy? You almost hit me." He noticed Sisto's partner had his right hand behind his back. *Calm yourself. Bad attitudes don't win gun fights.*

Sisto stood in front of him and pointed. "You told me you hurt your leg in an accident. American soldiers in Afghanistan drive motorcycles?"

On shit! Mike had hoped to keep his background secret. Few people had been told he was injured in Afghanistan. *Who's he been talking to, and what else does he know about me?* "The accident happened after I was shot and returned to America."

"Sure it did. What other lies are you telling me?"

Mike realized he needed to stick with his story, and his reaction had to reinforce his answer to Sisto's question. He paused and raised his voice. "You've seen my leg. Does it look like a bullet wound, or one that was crushed between a motorcycle and the bumper of a car?" He glared at Sisto. It was clear the Mafioso had not been anticipating his reply.

"Do you know who is stealing from me?"

"Hell no! I've paid each time you asked and told you there would be no problems. Why don't you ask the local Ndrangheta boss? The people in Vibo are complaining to him."

"Dante said you may not be able to pay. Be careful, American. Your asshole uncle had a bad attitude. You don't want to end up like he did."

Mike didn't back off and tapped his chest. "The Ndrangheta isn't shooting at me, Sisto. You may be the next name on their list."

Sisto stared at him. "I'm going to be watching you."

"Fine, go ahead." He tapped his left leg. "I don't move fast."

Sisto stepped closer. "If you are lying again, you won't make it back to America."

"I don't plan to go back anytime soon." Mike grinned. "No one wants to miss the battle between the Mafia and the Ndrangheta. Someone is a ghost with a pistol."

"You're full of shit," Sisto yelled.

Mike saluted. *If he was here to kill me, I'd be dead.* He limped away, got into his Jeep and focused on his hands clamped around the steering wheel. *Stay calm and act as if you don't give a shit.* He loosened his grip.

On his way back to the villa he became angrier as he thought about Sisto's threats. *He's an asshole, but Bortolo is the one giving the orders. I've got to get to the boss.*

###

As Mike parked in front of the house, Pio came out the door.

"Where have you been?" Pio asked.

"Looking at an olive grove ten kilometers from here. The owner may want to sell. Are you leaving?"

"Yes... going to the metal shop to pick up a part."

"Don't go yet. We need to talk."

Pio pointed to the chairs on the porch.

Mike told him what had happened on the way home.

"I talked to Imo last night," Pio said. "He told me nothing happens without Bortolo's orders. Sisto and his men don't dare piss him off."

"The boss is the key to this mess. Tell me everything Imo said."

"Each Sunday, Bortolo goes to his mother's house for lunch. Imo knows where it's located. It's a small villa on a large lot."

Mike glanced up and paused. "Are other homes near it?"

"No."

"Get the address. Let's take a trip this weekend to see if he visits her. We'll take the white van, but I need you to get license plates from Messina. Will that be a problem?"

"No. I can get them for a few euros."

CHAPTER XXII

MOM'S HOUSE

Saturday evening, Mike and Pio drove to a clump of trees on a hilltop west of Messina. Pio pulled under the canopy formed by the overhanging limbs and stopped.

Mike grabbed a canvas bag and jumped out. He walked to a tree trunk just over the crest of the hill and looked back. The van was not visible.

Pio joined him and pointed at a circular driveway in front of a brick and stone house at the base of the slope. "Imo told me that on Sundays he arrives at noon and parks near the front steps. He usually leaves before sunset."

Mike removed binoculars from the bag and handed them to Pio. He raised the rangefinder and focused on the center of the first step. "One thousand, fifteen meters. That accounts for the thirty meter drop from us to the front stairs. Since the front of the house is to our right, the car will be facing us."

Pio gazed through the field glasses. "Is that too far?"

Mike smiled. "No. If I can hit a jug of water from two and a half kilometers, I can easily put a bullet through his fat ass. Let's find a place to stay tonight, but not near Messina."

Pio looked to the side and mumbled something. He turned to Mike. "A town called Villafranca. It's on the coast an hour west of here. I've never been there, but I've heard it's nice. We don't want to pick a town where we'll be conspicuous."

The next afternoon Pio dropped Mike off at the base of the hill. "Call me when it's done. I'll pick you up here."

Mike, wore tan pants and a tan shirt to match the color of the terrain. He grabbed the canvas duffle bag from behind his seat and got out of the van. "This may take a few hours. If he's not there, I won't wait all afternoon for him. We'll have to think of something else." He pushed the door closed and headed up the hill.

At the crest, he picked a spot in a clump of bushes under a tree. He removed binoculars from the bag and focused on a black Mercedes parked in front of the house. Just as he had thought, the car faced him.

Mike assembled his rifle and set the empty duffel bag beside the weapon. He stretched out on the bag and positioned himself next to the sniper rifle.

For the next three and a half hours, he peered at the front of the house through the field glasses. *Back to doing what long shooters do. Lying still, visualizing the shot, and waiting for the target.*

At five-fifty, Bortolo walked out of the house with another man. *Damn it, he's not alone.* Mike set the binoculars beside the rifle and peered through the scope.

The two men stood talking on the landing. Bortolo tapped the man on the shoulder, hugged him and headed to his car. His friend went inside the house.

As Bortolo got behind the wheel, Mike slid the crosshairs to the rearview mirror. He slowed his breathing and exerted pressure on the trigger. The rifle recoiled against his shoulder.

An instant after the bullet passed through the windshield and took out the mirror, Bortolo raised both hands and ducked over the center console.

Mike moved the crosshairs to the driver's side mirror and fired a second shot. The mirror assembly shattered into pieces as it was torn from the door.

Time to move! Mike partially disassembled the rifle, shoved it into the bag, and raced down the backside of the hill.

He pulled his phone from his pocket and called Pio. "I'll be there in ten minutes. Pick me up at the side of the road."

###

Mike jumped into the van and Pio casually pulled back onto the road.

Pio, his eyes the size of golf balls, looked at him. "Is it done?"

"Yes. The first shot destroyed the rearview mirror, the second one ripped the driver's side mirror off the door."

Pio's eyebrows raised. "You missed him?"

Mike didn't hide his smile. "I hit what I aimed at. I only wanted him to shit his pants. If he dies, another boss, will take his place and nothing will change."

"You think he'll be frightened enough?"

"Not yet, but what just happened will be a vivid memory forever. I've got something else up my sleeve. He needs to realize the executioner, a ghost, can ruin his life at any time."

"What are we going to do next?"

"We'll send him a message... it needs to be done quickly. If he calls the police, they may find bullet fragments. If they do, they're going to realize the shooter was not close by."

Pio turned to him with a mischievous grin. "That could be to our advantage."

"How?"

"Bortolo will worry. The executioner doesn't need to walk up to him."

"You're right." Mike laughed. "His only choice is to stay behind closed doors, and stay away from windows, for the rest of his life. When we get to Vibo, I'll put something together to send to him."

CHAPTER XXIII

THE PROMISE

Back at Casa Anello, Mike had no intention of wasting time. He sat at the desk in his bedroom and stared at the laptop screen. He realized no threat would frighten the Mafia boss enough to make him stop. He bit his bottom lip and nodded. *Promise him something he can't live with.*

It took him two hours to find three photos, make a copy of a famous painting, and write something that would force Bortolo to rethink his protection money scheme.

He opened a blank page and began to type. Under his words he inserted a copy of the 1808 oil painting of Goddess Nemesis.

On the second page he wrote his demands.

Mike cut and pasted three photos onto separate pieces of paper and printed the document. He placed the five pages in a large envelope, but did not seal it.

Rachele's loud call startled him, "Lunch will be ready in five minutes."

In the living room, he spotted Pio tapping the screen of his cell phone. "You busy?"

Pio shoved the phone in his pocket. "No."

Mike pointed to large armchairs. "Let's sit, I have something to show you."

Pio dropped into a chair. "Is something wrong?"

"No. I think I found a way to make Bortolo quit stealing from us and the others." He removed the stapled pages from the envelope and handed them to him.

After studying the first two pages, Pio looked at Mike. "What is the painting?"

"It's Divine Vengeance, lighting the way with a torch, and Justice, armed with sword, as they pursue a murderer. It was painted by Pierre-Paul Prud'hon in 1808."

"I don't think this will scare him."

Mike smiled. "You have three more pages."

When Pio turned the page, his eyes widened, and he sat erect. At the sight of the next page he froze and looked at Mike.

"Continue, you have one page remaining," Mike said.

Pio's mouth dropped open, and he took a deep breath as he stared at the final sheet of paper. "I was wrong. He'll do everything you ask." He handed the document back to Mike.

"Come and eat," Rachele called from the kitchen.

CHAPTER XXIV

REALITY

Bortolo parked the silver Alfa Romeo Giulia in front of *Lo Spirito* and turned off the engine. He raised his unsteady right hand, stared at it, and then rubbed the stitches on his forehead. *I'm lucky the glass didn't hit me in the eye.* He grabbed his cane.

Inside the bar, he approached a man behind the gelato counter. "Where's the envelope?"

"On your table." The guy pointed to the back of the room.

He walked to his favorite table, sat and picked up the large envelope. Centered on one side was his full name written in bold cursive. *Whoever did this, the nuns taught him well.* The back of the envelope was blank.

He slid a knife from his pocket, opened the envelope and laid the stapled pages in front of him.

One of his men set a demitasse of coffee on the table. "Do you want pastry or bread?"

"No. A small glass of Sambuca." He stared at the words typed in bold letters and began to read aloud.

"Come Nemesis. A message from the goddess of divine retribution and revenge. Behold on wrongs swift vengeance waits and art subdues the strong."

Below the words was a photo of a painting showing two winged figures above a dead body, and a man running away. *Who the hell is Nemesis and why the old art?* He turned the page and continued reading out loud.

"I hit the mirrors of your car because they are what I was aiming at. It is much easier to put a bullet in your head, but no more of your men will die and I will not kill you. You have seventy-two hours to do what I say."

Bortolo bit his bottom lip. *No one tells me what to do!* He moved to the next line.

"Stop demanding protection money from the people of Calabria. Get your men out and never return to Vibo Valentia. Sell *Antonio Garage* back to the family you stole it from. The equipment and products in the store will be included. Ten euros will be your selling price. If you ignore me, and let three days pass, I will methodically begin to take from you the things you cherish most."

He slammed his fist against the table. "You think you frighten me! I will personally come to Vibo and kill you!"

His loud outburst caused everyone on the bar to quit talking. He glanced around the room, turned back to the papers in front of him and turned the page.

Centered on the paper was a photo of a man standing on a beach. His right arm had been amputated. Typed below the photo were the words, "Imagine life with one arm." He yanked his hands away from papers and his eyes narrowed.

Bortolo turned to the next page and looked at a photo of a man in a wheelchair. He had only one leg and one arm. His eyes moved to the caption below the picture. "Imagine life with one leg and one arm." He shifted in his chair and gazed at his trembling hands.

When he looked at the last page, he read what was written above a solid black square. "This is what a blind man sees."

"Who delivered this envelope?" he yelled.

The man at the gelato counter ran to him. "No one. It was on the floor near the door when we arrived this morning."

"What time is it?" Bortolo asked.

The man glanced at his watch. "Ten-thirty. Is something wrong?"

"No. Is Sisto in Messina?"

"Yes."

"Call him. I want him here now."

CHAPTER XXV

THE WAIT

A day and a half had passed since the envelope was delivered to Bortolo's bar in Messina.

Mike sat in the living room contemplating what the Mafia boss may do next. *Is this guy going to get off his ass or is he an arrogant bastard? Don't make me kill you.*

Pio walked in the front door. "What are you doing?"

Mike shook his head. "Waiting for our friend to make the next move."

Pio sat across from him. "He has to be frightened to death... but I'm not an expert on Mafia behavior."

"It's not that Enzo and the other two guys didn't deserve their trip to hell, but we can't continue," Mike said. "I don't want to kill any more of them."

"You did what had to be done. Sooner or later, Gina, you, and I would end up on their list. If he does what you ask, how will you know?"

Mike pressed his lips together and shook his head. "I don't know. What's the name of the bar where Imo works?"

"Stromboli."

Mike stood. "Let's go talk to him, ask if he's heard anything."

Pio held up his hand. "Wait. What if Sisto and his friends are there? They don't know he's married to my niece."

"You're right," Mike said. "Do you have his phone number?"

"Yes, I'll call." Pio tapped the screen of his phone and spent a minute talking to Imo. When he ended the call, he turned to Mike. "He said Sisto was there last night. He told Imo the boss wanted him and his men to return to Sicily."

"Did he say why?"

"No."

"Let's go to lunch in Vibo. After we eat, we'll drive around town. We may spot him or his friends."

After they finished eating pizza at a local restaurant, Mike and Pio spent the next three hours driving through town looking for Bortolo's men.

Late that afternoon they headed back to Casa Anello. As they passed *Antonio Garage,* Pio grabbed Mike's arm and yelled. "Stop! Turn around and go back!"

"Back where?"

"*Antonio Garage!*"

"Why?"

"The man who killed himself... his son was standing out front."

Mike swung to the shoulder and made a U-turn. He pulled in front of the garage and parked near the man. No lights were on in the building and the business seemed to be closed.

The guy waved at Pio and approached the Jeep as they got out. "Hello, Pio. Nice to see you again," he said with a broad smile.

Pio shook the man's hand and turned to Mike. "This is Rico... Rico, this is Mike Anello, Gina's cousin. His father was Romeo's brother."

Rico shook Mike's hand. "Romeo's death was a sad day in Vibo."

Mike nodded. "So was the passing of your father."

"What are you doing here at the garage," Pio asked.

Rico smiled, pulled a folded paper from his shirt pocket and handed it to Pio. "A man delivered this to me two hours ago."

Pio read and his smile grew. He handed it to Mike.

Mike read aloud. "An agreement has been reached to sell *Antonio Garage* to you for a price of ten euros. Contact Gianmichele Alivio, an attorney in Vibo Valentia."

Rico held up a key. "This unlocks the front door."

Adrenaline shot through Mike's body and his heart drummed in his chest. He glanced at Pio and clamped his

191

mouth closed to keep from laughing as he handed the paper back to Rico. "What happened... was anything more said?

"No." He shrugged. "I have ten euros and an appointment with the attorney tomorrow at nine. He told me the sales agreement would be typed, and the garage would be mine. I'm going to pray it goes well. I won't ask questions."

Pio tapped him on the arm. "Maybe the police found out something and people will now go to jail."

"I'll bet you're right," Mike said. "Once the Carabinieri started investigating the murders, the Sicilians got scared. But that doesn't mean they'll stop stealing from us."

"They'll never get another euro from my family. I'll keep a shotgun in the store."

Pio held up a hand. "Don't say that too loud. The police may think you had something to do with the men being shot."

Mike looked at Rico and then raised a finger to his lips. "Do what you must, but tell no one."

###

By the time Mike and Pio returned to Casa Anello, they were ready to celebrate. Mike pulled out a bottle of Vecchia Romagna Brandy and they sat in the living room drinking and toasting each other.

Pio raised his glass. "To the future and the expansion of Casa Anello Olive Oil."

Both took a long drink.

"I hope we're not toasting too soon," Mike said. "Bortolo may still want more."

"After looking at the photos of people with missing limbs, do you think he's that stupid?"

"I hope not. I'd rather practice shooting at targets that don't bleed."

CHAPTER XXVI

TREPIDATION

For the fourth day since he'd received the envelope, Bortolo sat on his couch and stared at the stapled pages on the coffee table. Dying had never scared him. Anyone who chose the life he had could only surround himself with loyal followers and protect himself with bodyguards. But still death could come. Becoming incapacitated and weak frightened him more than death. He would be alive to watch everything he had worked for ripped from him by vultures wanting to take over his organization. He would live to see his family robbed of their fortune. To see them forced into poverty while he could do nothing to help. *I'd rather die with honor.*

Over and over again he had asked himself the same question. *How do you hide from a madman who could be a kilometer away? Someone you can't see and don't know is there.*

The fear of being shot without seeing his attacker, or feeling pain before he heard the crack of a rifle, consumed the hours of his day. At night dreams of an acid attack, and opening his eyes to darkness, jarred him awake. He jumped when his cell phone rang. "Hello."

He listened to Sisto's voice.

"No. I'm not coming to the bar, and I don't want you or anyone else to go back to Vibo. The clans have paid their debt. There will be no more protection money from Calabria."

The more Sisto talked and pressed the issue, the more Bortolo tightened his grip on the phone. "Sisto! If you can't do what I say, I'll find someone who can! There are many men who would kill to take your place." He ended the call, leapt from the couch, and walked to the French doors leading to the balcony.

Through the glass panes he watched a woman, in the building across the street, sweep her balcony. His eyes rose to the top of the structure and he froze. A sharp pain flashed across his chest and he suddenly felt claustrophobic. A man, dressed in black, stood on the roof looking in his direction.

Bortolo jumped to the side, knocking over a lamp. He regained his balance, slammed the interior shutters to block what he had seen, and sat in a chair in the corner of the room. His hand trembled as he wiped perspiration from his forehead. "Please, God," he whimpered. "Don't let him take my eyes. I'll never go to Vibo again."

CHAPTER XXVII

THE FUTURE

A week after he heard the news about *Antonio Garage* being returned to its original owners, Mike sat at the kitchen table eating freshly baked cookies and drinking coffee with Adria.

He had not told anyone of his decision to stay in Italy. *I need to call Bob.* He glanced at his watch.

"Are you bored?" Adria asked.

He took her hand. "No moment with you could ever be boring. I'm thinking of when Casa Anello can begin buying more olive groves."

Adria leaned to him. "Relax. Everything here moves much slower than it does in America."

He smiled and squeezed her hand. "You're right. Let's go look at your new office."

As they walked hand in hand to a two-story metal building half the size of the sprawling villa, Mike couldn't take his eyes off her. Although she didn't need to wear business attire, Adria looked as if she was strolling to her office in a large corporate headquarters. She wore a tailored pinstriped suit with a sheer white collarless blouse. The pencil skirt hugged her trim silhouette.

"You didn't need to wear a suit... jeans and a T-shirt would have been okay."

She stopped, turned to face him, and grinned. "I dressed to impress the boss."

"It worked." He kissed her cheek.

At eight-thirty that evening, Mike and Pio sat on the front porch waiting for dinner.

"How are we going to get the money back to the other people?" Mike asked.

Pio smiled. "I've got an idea, but it's going to cost us."

"What is it?"

"The old priest at Saint Michele's Church."

Mike furrowed his brow. The last thing he wanted was for a priest to find out where the money came from. "You haven't talked to him yet, have you?"

"No, and I won't. He's retiring in two months and wants to visit the Holy Land. I can arrange for him to receive the envelopes and instructions detailing what to do with them."

Mike took a deep breath. "Can he be trusted not to say anything?"

Pio nodded. "I've known him since I was a boy. We'll tell him people are waiting for their envelopes and give him a donation to help pay for his retirement trip."

Mike paused and stared at him. "I don't want him to know any of it came from us."

"That won't be a problem. I can arrange to have everything delivered to his apartment when he's not there."

Mike nodded and glanced at the floor. *How do we keep people from talking when they suddenly get their money back?* He turned to Pio. "If everyone is told to keep their mouths shut, will they?"

Pio grinned. "People around here are frightened of the Mafia and the Financial Police. They won't want the *tax terrorist* to discover they received a lot of cash. They'll hide it under a mattress."

"Good." Mike removed the phone from his pocket. "I have to contact a friend in Colorado."

"I'll call you when dinner is ready." Pio went into the house.

Mike tapped Bob Keal's name on the screen of his phone.

Bob's wife answered on the second ring. "Hello."

"Hi, Julie, it's Mike."

"Hi, is everything okay?"

"Everything is fine. Is Bob there?"

"Yes. He's staring at me with his hand out... hold on a second."

"Well, I'll be damned. How you doing and how is the olive oil business?"

"Great, how are you and Julie?"

"We're both fine. She's been bugging me, wanting to know when you're coming home. She has a new nurse waiting to meet you... a girl from Finland."

Mike laughed. "No Swedes available?"

"No, but this one is a knock-out."

"My loss," Mike said. "Listen, I need a favor."

"Sure, what?"

"Sell all of my guns, I won't be coming back for a while. Keep a thousand for yourself and take Julie out for dinner. Whatever is left, I want to donate to the Special Operations Warrior Foundation."

"You sure?"

"Yup. Tell Julie every drop of olive oil she needs, for the rest of her life, is on me. And tell the beautiful Miss Finland Mike Anello met someone."

"Damn, she'll be crushed. Julie told her you were Superman, standing up and lying down."

Mike wasn't sure how to respond. "That's... well... something your wife wouldn't know."

"Yes, she would. She had a long conversation with the two Russian roommates you dumped before you left."

Mike laughed. "Ever since the Soviet Union went down the tubes, the Russians can't keep anything secret."

Pio opened the door. "Dinner is ready."

Mike wanted to continue the conversation, but couldn't keep the others waiting. "Food's on the table. I'll call you in a day or so."

When Mike walked into the dining room, Pio, his wife Camilla, Gina and Adria were seated at the table. He sat in the vacant chair at one end.

Gina passed the large antipasto plate to Adria. "Are you going to stay at your parents' apartment?"

"I would, but my old bedroom is small." She shrugged. "I should look for a one-bedroom apartment I can rent."

Gina waved a hand. "No. Move into my father's old room. It's quite large and you can decorate it however you like."

Mike smiled. *My cousin comes up with the best ideas.* He glanced at Pio, raised his eyebrows, and turned to Adria. "You'll be able to walk to work."

"And you'll be close to loving friends," Gina said.

Mike winked at her. "Yes she will."

Adria paused and he could see she was fighting to hide a smile.

"Mike may be a little intimidated." She looked at him.

Mike rubbed his hands together and grinned. "I'd love to find out what that feels like."

THE END